The Riddle of the
Hidden Treasure

Enid Blyton

The Riddle of the Hidden Treasure

AWARD PUBLICATIONS LIMITED

This book was first published in Great Britain
under the title *The Treasure Hunters* by Newnes Ltd
in 1940. It was updated and altered to become part
of the Riddle series in 1997 by Enid Blyton's
daughter, Gillian Baverstock.

For further information on Enid Blyton
please visit *www.blyton.com*

ISBN 978-1-84135-741-6

Illustrated by Patricia Ludlow
Cover illustration by Gavin Rowe

First published 1940 as *The Treasure Hunters*
Revised edition published 1997 as *The Riddle of the Hidden Treasure*
First published by Award Publications Limited 2004 as
The Young Adventurers and the Hidden Treasure
This edition entitled *The Riddle of the Hidden Treasure*
first published 2009

Published by Award Publications Limited,
The Old Riding School, The Welbeck Estate,
Worksop, Nottinghamshire, S80 3LR

12 3

Printed in the United Kingdom

CONTENTS

1. Gran's Old House   7
2. The Greylings Treasure   18
3. Adventure in the Woods   28
4. The Secret Little House   39
5. The House has a Spring-Clean   48
6. A Most Exciting Discovery   58
7. Mr Pots-of-Money   69
8. Where is the Winding Road?   79
9. A Visit to the Taylors' Farm   86
10. Someone Else is Treasure Hunting!   95
11. The Children Follow the Map   106
12. Russet is a Great Help!   115
13. Mr Potts is Clever   125
14. An Exciting Morning   134
15. An Unexpected Punishment   145
16. An Underground Adventure   155
17. The Treasure at Last!   164
18. Safe at the Taylors' Farm   175
19. Good Luck to Greylings!   183

CHAPTER 1

GRAN'S OLD HOUSE

Nick was sticking some stamps into his album when Laura and Katie came tearing into the playroom.

"Nick! What do you think? We're going to stay with Gran and Grandad in their old manor house!" cried Laura.

"Really?" said Nick, surprised and pleased. "How do you know?"

"Because Uncle Peter said so," Katie said happily. "Isn't that lovely? Laura's told us so much about it that I feel as if I know their house already, even though we've never been there."

Nick and Katie had lost their parents in a car crash more than a year ago. At first they had been looked after by an aunt who didn't want them, and an uncle who was too weak to stand up for them. Rather than be taken into care, the two children had run away and camped out in a hollow tree in

7

the middle of a nearby wood, living on food brought by Laura and her dog, Russet. Eventually, when Laura became ill, they were discovered, but Laura's parents took Nick and Katie into their own home and Laura, who had been an only child, was delighted. Nothing could ever replace their own mother and father, but Aunt Marion and Uncle Peter, as Nick and Katie called Laura's parents, made them feel they belonged to a loving family once more.

Laura's mother came into the room, and smiled at the three excited faces.

"Laura's told you about Gran's invitation, I see. It'll be fun for you to stay with them over half-term. Gran and Grandad are very kind and you'll be happy with them while Dad and I go away for a holiday. The doctor says I must have a rest after having flu so badly."

"Let me see their letter, Mum!" begged Laura. She took it and read out loud:

"'It'll be lovely to have the three children to stay with us, especially as this may be the last time they can come here. It looks as though we have at last found a buyer for the house, though it will almost break our hearts to leave this beautiful place.'"

"Oh Mum!" said Laura, looking up in dismay. "Are they really leaving Greylings Manor? I thought Dad said it would be his and then mine some day."

"Yes, we thought so too," said her mother. "But you see, things have been very difficult lately for Gran and Grandad, living on his pension. They really can't afford to stay in such a big house with all the expenses of looking after it. They have to sell it, and find a smaller house."

"Oh, poor Gran and Grandad," said Katie. "They must be feeling very unhappy about it."

"When are we going, Mum?" asked Laura.

"You haven't long to wait," said Laura's mother. "You're going tomorrow! So I'll be very busy today, packing for you all."

"Oh, Mum! What about Russet? We can't leave him behind! Hasn't Gran asked him too?"

Her mother smiled. "Well," she said, "Gran says that as he's much better behaved than he used to be, he can come!"

"Great!" said Laura. "Did you hear that,

Russet? You're going on holiday too!"

"Woof, woof," barked Russet, sensing the excitement and determined not to let Laura out of his sight.

The next day came very quickly, and in no time at all the three children were packed into the car, with the luggage in the boot, and off they went.

"You'll love Gran's old house," said Laura, as they sped along. "It's the sort of place where all kinds of things have happened, and where you feel anything might still happen."

"Oh, I do like places like that," said Katie, happily. "Are there good walks around, Laura?"

"Most exciting ones," said Laura. "There's a deep, mysterious wood nearby, where we can go exploring. A stream flows through the wood, making part of it very marshy, and there's a farm nearby where Mr Taylor lives with his wife who makes the most delicious cakes."

"It sounds great!" said Katie. "Nick's brought his binoculars and I've got my flower press with me. We ought to find plenty of birds and flowers."

"Russet's going to enjoy all the new walks," said Nick. "I'm so glad we could bring him too."

Laura's mother agreed. "Rags, Granny's dog, died last year, and she only has her cat, Whiskers, now. I'd feel happier if you have Russet with you while you're walking in the woods," she said. "After last year, I don't want anyone getting lost again! Just make sure that Russet doesn't get over-excited in the house."

"And I hope you'll remember to be quiet and well-behaved in the house," said Uncle Peter. "Gran and Grandad have had a lot of problems lately, and it's kind of them to have you."

"We won't cause any trouble, Uncle Peter," said Nick. "We'll do everything we can to help."

"We really will do our best," promised Katie.

"We're nearly there!" said Laura's mother. "Look, there's the wood Laura was telling you about."

The children pressed their noses against the car window and peered out. They saw a thick, dark wood with one or two narrow paths running into it. It looked very exciting.

The car turned into a drive between two big gateposts. On top of each stood a stone eagle.

"We're here, we're here!" shouted Laura.

The car went up a winding drive and stopped in front of a lovely house. It was long and rather low, with very tall chimneys. The windows had leaded panes, and the sides of the house came out to form a sunny courtyard, in which walked some white fantail pigeons.

"Isn't it lovely!" said Katie, jumping out of the car. The old house glowed red in the sunshine and seemed to welcome the children.

"Gran! There's Gran!" cried Laura, and she ran to meet the old lady who stood on the steps to greet them. She was small and round and smiling, and she wore her wavy white hair done up in a soft bun.

Grandad came up behind her. He had a pointed white beard and a thick mop of silvery hair. He hurried down the steps to kiss Laura's mother.

"Welcome to Greylings Manor!" he said

to them all. "It may be the last time we welcome you here, but we hope it'll be the happiest!"

Laura hugged her grandmother and kissed her grandfather. Nick and Katie hung back, not quite knowing what to do. Laura's grandmother gave them both a hug and her grandfather shook hands with them. "It's lovely to welcome you both here and I hope you'll have a wonderful holiday," he said, smiling. "It'll be so much nicer for Laura not to be on her own all the time."

"What an amazing place!" said Nick, as they went up to their rooms, followed by Russet, who was enjoying all the new smells.

"We've been given the two little rooms up in the roof," said Laura.

She opened a door and the others went in. They found themselves in a low-roofed room, with latticed windows that looked out on to the sunny garden at the back of the house. The walls of the room were crooked, the ceiling was crooked, and the big beams that ran here and there were crooked too!

"It's like a room in a fairytale!" said Katie, delighted. "I love the whitewashed walls and the uneven floor. Whose room is this?"

"It's our room," said Laura. "Nick has the little room that leads off it. Open that low door in the corner and you'll see your room, Nick."

Nick opened a low door that came no higher than his shoulder. He stooped and went through it. He came into a small room that was almost round, with a ceiling that sloped right down to the floor on one side, and two tiny windows that let in the sun. A white pigeon sat on a small slanting roof outside one window, and cooed softly.

"It's brilliant!" said Nick. "It's like a room forgotten by time."

They washed, and then went downstairs. Laura's parents were out in the garden talking to Gran and Grandad.

"They won't want to be disturbed," said Laura. "Come on, I'll show you the rest of the house!"

Nick, Katie and Russet followed her. It was the most exciting house imaginable. For one thing there were three separate staircases! One was the main one, a wide, curving flight that went from the big landing to the hall. Another led from the kitchens to the attics, and a third, the most mysterious, led from a door in the dining-room, behind the wall, and up to the children's rooms, entering Nick's room unexpectedly from a cupboard!

"How fantastic!" said Nick as he went up the tiny stairway, so narrow and dark, and came out of the little cupboard in his own room. Russet followed him up, looking very surprised.

There were old family portraits to see: Great-Grandfather, looking rather stern; Great-Great-Grandmother, looking very pretty indeed in a blue bonnet, staring at them from her frame.

"She's like you, Laura," said Nick, and so she was. She had just the same deep blue eyes and fair hair, and the same happy smile on her lips.

They were still looking at the pictures when Gran called them.

"Your mother and father are leaving now!" she called. "Come and say goodbye."

The children ran downstairs. They all

hugged Laura's parents, wished them a lovely holiday, and then watched them get back into the car. Uncle Peter started the engine and called to them.

"Be good now! We'll write to you!"

"Goodbye, children!" cried Laura's mother, and she waved her hand. The car swept down the drive and disappeared out of the eagle-flanked gates. They were gone!

"It's the start of our holiday!" cried Laura, and she jumped up and down the steps. She turned to Gran.

"Where's Whiskers?" she asked. "We ought to introduce him to Russet."

At that moment, a large black cat walked slowly round the corner and, ignoring Russet, rubbed himself first round Gran's legs and then round Laura's. Russet rushed at him, barking loudly. Nick grabbed his collar, but Whiskers was quite unperturbed. He turned round and spat at Russet very rudely. Russet promptly backed away, remembering how Tiger, Laura's cat, had clawed his nose when he was a puppy.

"Now then, Russet, no cat-chasing at Greylings Manor," said Grandad, bending down to stroke him. "Still, it's nice to have a dog around the place again. I miss our old Rags."

"Woof!" said Russet, rolling over on his back with all four paws in the air.

"Ridiculous dog!" said Grandad, tickling him with his foot. "Now, let's go and find some lunch. I'm sure we could all do with something to eat."

Indoors they all went, and took their places in the long, low dining-room. Russet lay down on Laura's foot. He was just as happy as the children!

CHAPTER 2

THE GREYLINGS TREASURE

For the next few days the children and
Russet had a fine time, tearing round the
garden, going into all the sheds and
outbuildings, eating peas in the kitchen
garden, and hunting for ripening
strawberries.

Sometimes Whiskers, the big black cat,
sauntered along beside them. The fantail
pigeons disappeared like a cloud of
snowflakes when they saw Whiskers, but at
other times they were tame and would come
flying down and perch on the children's
shoulders and hands. Russet soon got used
to Whiskers, but he barked furiously at the
pigeons when they flew down to the
children.

"This is such a beautiful place," said
Laura, looking back at the old house as she
went out of the little white gate that led to
the kitchen garden. "How I wish that Gran

and Grandad could go on living here, and that it would be Dad's later on, and mine too, when I'm grown up."

"Look! There's a car coming up the drive!" interrupted Nick. The three children watched to see who was arriving.

The car's driver, wearing a peaked cap, got out and opened the rear door of the car. A very smartly dressed lady appeared, followed by a tall man. They went up the steps to the front door.

The children went into the kitchen garden as soon as the visitors disappeared into the house. They thought no more about them until later on in the morning.

Laura was playing hide-and-seek with the others. She had gone into a little hedged garden that Gran called her own. In it she had planted all her favourite flowers, and here the pigeons came to be fed each day.

Laura pushed her way into the middle of the thick yew hedge. She was sure that the others would never think of looking for her there! She stayed quite still, and waited for the other two to find her.

While she was there, Gran came into the

garden. She sat down on her white seat, and looked into her little pond, where white waterlilies were showing.

Laura thought at first that Gran's footsteps were those of Katie and Nick, and she kept as quiet as could be. But when the footsteps stopped, and nobody spoke or called, she carefully parted the green boughs and peeped to see who was there.

"Oh! It's only Gran!" she thought. And then she had a shock.

Gran was crying! Tears ran down her cheeks, and she mopped them up with a tiny lace handkerchief. Laura stared in horror. She had never seen a grown-up cry before, and it was dreadful to see tears rolling down Gran's cheeks. Whatever could be making her so unhappy?

She struggled out of the hedge at once. Gran heard her, wiped her eyes quickly, and then looked round in surprise. She tried to smile when she saw the hot, dirty face peeping out of the hedge.

"Oh, Laura dear!" she said. "You did make me jump! Are you playing hide-and-seek?"

"Yes," said Laura. She ran up to her

grandmother. "What's the matter?" she asked. "Why are you crying? Has somebody been unkind to you? Just wait till I see them, that's all!"

She looked so fierce that Gran couldn't help laughing, though she still had tears in her eyes.

"No," she said. "Nobody's been unkind. But did you see those visitors this morning, Laura?"

"Yes," said Laura. "Did they make you cry?"

"In a way they did," said Gran. "You see, they came to look at Greylings Manor, because they are thinking of buying it, and it made me feel sad to think that Grandad and I will have to go. It has always belonged to the Greyling family, and now it must go to strangers. Poor old house – it won't like that!"

"But Gran, have you lost all your money?" asked Laura. "Why must you suddenly go?"

"We haven't suddenly lost our money," said Gran. "The family have been unlucky, as the years went by. First, the Greylings Treasure was lost."

"The Greylings Treasure!" exclaimed Laura, excited. "What's that? I've never heard of it!"

"Here she is!" Katie's voice suddenly cried, and she came running into Gran's hedged garden. "She isn't even hiding. Catch her!"

"No, Katie, don't," said Laura. "I'm not playing now. Gran is telling me about something exciting called the Greylings Treasure!"

"Whatever's that?" said Katie and Nick in surprise. They came to sit beside Gran on the white seat. The old lady went on with her story.

"Well," she said, "over four hundred years ago an adventurous young man called Hugh Greyling joined the Navy. One day he came home with a chest full of treasure and gold that he'd won fighting a Spanish galleon. This made him a very wealthy man, so he bought land here, built Greylings Manor and settled down with his family. The Greylings Treasure remained with the family for nearly a hundred years, carefully guarded and with only the eldest son being told where it was hidden."

"What was the treasure?" asked Laura.

"The chest contained strings of pearls, diamonds set in marvellous metals, a golden cup studded with rubies and sapphires, and other small things," said Gran. "There is a book all about the treasure in the library."

"I must read it!" said Nick, fascinated.

"Well," said Gran, "this treasure was in the Greyling family for many years, and then civil war broke out. You know what civil war is, don't you?"

"It's a war when a country fights against itself," said Nick. "Families against families. My father said it's the worst of all wars."

"It is," said Gran. "Well, during this civil war the Greyling family was afraid that their enemies would steal the treasure. So Peter Greyling, the eldest son, who had the same name as your father, Laura, and was very like him to look at, took the treasure to hide it away safely. He left the house with it and never came back!"

"What happened to him?" asked Katie, in surprise.

"Nobody knows," said Gran. "We think

he was killed by his enemies. But the treasure was never found, or heard of again."

"Where do you think it went?" asked Nick.

"Either Peter Greyling hid it in some very secret place where it was never found, and then died before he could tell anyone about it, or else his enemies took it and kept it for themselves," said Gran. "But I don't think that happened, because somebody would have seen the treasure, and sooner or later it would have been talked about."

"Oh Gran! Do you mean to say that you think it's still hidden somewhere?" asked Laura in astonishment.

"I sometimes think so," said Gran. "Tradition had it that as long as the Greyling family drank out of the golden cup once a year, good fortune, good health, and happiness would remain with them but if the cup passed out of the family, then these gifts would disappear too."

"It sounds like a fairytale," said Laura, who loved magic and mystery. "Gran, did the tale come true?"

"Well, in a way it did," said Gran. "I don't believe in these old sayings of good and bad luck, you know, but ever since the treasure went, the Greylings have been unlucky. They've lost their money through the years, and they've had illness and sorrow, and now Grandad and I have so little money left that we must leave the old manor house and live elsewhere."

"Wait a little longer till I'm grown-up, and I'll earn enough money for you to stay here!" cried Laura.

"I'm afraid we can't wait as long as that, Laura," said Gran, putting her arm round her. "We shall have to go before Christmas. Those people who came today have offered to buy the house at a good price, and also to take the two farms that go with it."

"Four hundred years in the same family," said Nick, looking at the old house with its tall chimneys. "I'd hate to think it wouldn't be Greylings any more. If only we had that treasure now, Gran! Then you could stay here, and not worry any more."

"I'd like to see that book that tells us about the treasure," said Laura.

"I'll show it to you when you go indoors," said Gran.

So that evening the three children pored over the old book which contained the pictures of the Greylings Treasure. The golden cup was clearly illustrated and the children looked at it in admiration. It had precious stones set around the middle, and the base was covered with them. The picture was in colour, and the cup shone as if the stones were real!

The children could not understand the writing in the book, for the lettering was very old, and had faded with the years. They looked at the pictures of great brooches and necklaces and pins, and wished they all belonged to the family now.

"It's the most exciting story I've heard," said Laura. "Gran, I feel as if I must go hunting for the lost treasure straight away!"

"Many people have searched," said Gran, with a smile. "But nobody has found it. I'm afraid it was stolen years ago, and then sold. It's gone for ever now."

But Laura wouldn't let herself think that. She loved to imagine all kinds of things. "I'll pretend it can be found!" she said. "I'll go searching for it every day! I'll be a treasure hunter!"

"We will, too," said Katie and Nick. "It will make exploring everything even more fun!"

CHAPTER 3

ADVENTURE IN THE WOODS

Nick didn't really take the treasure hunt seriously, but Katie and Laura did. They tapped the walls of the old house to see if they could find hollow places behind which treasure might be hidden. They went into the attics and got themselves covered with the dust and cobwebs they found in every corner.

"Look," said Nick at last, "if the treasure were here, it would have been discovered by now. Gran says there was only one secret passage, and that was the staircase to my room, which was found and opened years ago. And Uncle Peter must have looked everywhere when he was a boy."

"Children, you really must go outside," called Gran. "It's far too nice a day for you to spend in the house."

"But Gran, we're treasure-hunting!" cried Laura.

"Well, you must hunt outside," said Gran. "Go on, out of the house, all of you!"

So the three children had to go out of the house and they wandered over to the gate of the kitchen garden. Mr Tetley, the gardener, was there and he waved them away.

"Don't you come in here this morning!" he shouted. "You ate half a row of my best peas yesterday and you can keep out today!"

"Bother!" said Katie. "I just felt like a few peas. What shall we do?"

"Let's go treasure-hunting in the woods!" said Laura eagerly. "We haven't been there yet. We could follow one of those little paths and see where it leads to."

"We'll have to be careful," said Nick. "The woods are so big, we might get lost."

"Well, Russet's coming too," said Laura, "and he always knows the way home. Come on, Russet. We're going hunting! Treasure-hunting, Russet!"

"Woof, woof!" said Russet, thinking that Laura meant rabbit-hunting. So all four of them set off. They went down the drive and out of the eagle gates. They turned to the left and soon came to the woods.

They went in under the trees. There was

a greenish light in the wood, very cool and lovely. The trees were so thick overhead that only tiny specks of sunlight filtered through, lying like pieces of gold on the ground below.

Rabbit paths ran everywhere. Russet rushed excitedly about, following first one and then another. The children followed quite a wide one, thinking it was a real path, but it wasn't. It stopped at a big rabbit hole and Russet almost disappeared down it, barking in excitement. The children had to pull him out.

"Well, we can't go down the hole," said Nick. "That's where the path leads to. Where shall we go now?"

"Let's go deeper into the woods," said Laura. "It feels dark and mysterious. You don't know what we might find!"

"Well, you won't find the little people, if that's what you're thinking of," said Nick, laughing.

"Listen, what's that noise?" said Katie, stopping suddenly. They all stood still. There was a rushing noise that was not the sound of the wind in the trees.

"It sounds like water," said Laura,

puzzled. "Oh, of course! I told you there was a stream that ran through the woods, didn't I? It wanders here and there, so perhaps we're near it."

She walked between the tall trees. The ground became rather wet and marshy, and the children had to tread carefully.

"There it is!" said Nick at last. He pointed to where a dark green stream flowed swiftly along between overgrown banks. The children went over to it.

"It looks very deep," Katie said. "Let's walk along beside it. I'd like to see where it goes."

So they followed the stream. It was difficult, because bushes grew so thickly on the bank in some places that they had to leave the stream, make a detour and then come back to the water again.

The stream grew wider and shallower as they followed its banks deeper into the woods. It lost its green colour and became brown. It bubbled and gurgled, and in its depths quick fishes darted about.

Then suddenly the stream widened out into a large pool, like a small lake, before flowing out again at the other end.

"Isn't it lovely!" said Katie in surprise. "I wonder how it turned itself into a pond. It looks so round that you'd think it had been made by someone."

"Whoever would excavate a lake in the middle of a wood?" said Nick scornfully. "Ooh, look! What a marvellous waterlily that is!"

Waterlilies covered the pond. Wild yellow ones grew there, but deep red and paler pink ones lay on the water also.

"I wish I could pick that crimson lily and take it back for Gran," said Laura, looking at the one that Nick had pointed to.

"It's deep," said Katie, looking into the water. "You couldn't paddle out to it."

Nick made his way round the pond, looking to see if there was any shallower place. "There's a big flat rock here," he said. "And another under the water. I might be able to stand on that and reach it."

The flat rock was green with slime. Nick stood carefully on it, barefooted, and then stepped on to the flat stone below. He felt about with his foot and said, "I do believe there's another flat stone below this one as well. Just like steps!"

"They *are* steps!" said Katie in surprise. She had scraped the green slime off with a stone, and below the slime was white marble! "Look, Nick, they are real steps. Steps that somebody put here for the pond."

Nick stared down in surprise. Katie was right. Nick forgot all about the red water-lily and began to scrape the steps as well.

"Why on earth should anyone build steps here?" he said. "You only put marble steps by a pond if you want to feed swans, or go boating, or sit in a sheltered place and look at the water."

"Swans wouldn't come here," said Katie. "They like more open water. And there aren't any boats."

"No, but there might have been once," said Nick. "Hey! I wonder if there was once a summerhouse or a boathouse near here. After all, if somebody took the trouble to build the marble steps, they might have built a little summerhouse for themselves as well!"

"Let's look!" said Laura. So the three children began to hunt around the pond. The trees and bushes were so thick that it was difficult to push through them.

Suddenly Katie gave a shout. "Look here! What do you think this is?"

Nick and Laura scrambled over to where Katie was standing. She was pulling at some thick ivy.

"Look," she said. "There's brick under this ivy. I believe the ivy, the brambles and the honeysuckle have grown all together here, and hidden a building of some sort!"

Laura and Nick peered about excitedly. It certainly seemed as if the great bramble and ivy cluster might be growing over something, but they couldn't see any sign of a building there.

"It's like the castle in Sleeping Beauty," said Laura, "all overgrown with thorns. Oh, look, look!"

Nick and Katie looked. Russet had gone after a rabbit, and had scraped hard at the bottom of the great ivy tangle. Where he had scraped, stone steps showed, steps that must lead down to the pond!

"So there must be some sort of a building beneath this tangle of bushes!" cried Nick. "Steps wouldn't lead down from nothing. There must have been a tiny house of some sort here, with steps leading down to the pool. However can we find out?"

"We'll have to borrow an axe from Mr Tetley," said Laura excitedly. "Then we can chop away the ivy and brambles and see what's underneath."

"Well, there won't be a Sleeping Beauty inside, so don't hope for that, Laura!" said Nick, grinning. "I expect it's just a tumbledown hut built by somebody who loved to come and dream in the woods."

"Let's go back and get an axe now, at once," begged Katie. "Look, when I pull away the ivy here, there's more stone or brick underneath. I know there's a secret house here."

"All right," said Nick, who was longing to find out more himself. "We'll go back now, this very minute."

So back they went, making their way over the marshy ground. They would never have taken the right path if Russet hadn't shown them the way! But he trotted ahead, sniffing, and soon led them to the rabbit path they had first followed.

When they were out of the woods, they ran along the lane, up the drive and into Mr

Tetley's garden shed. He was there, potting plants.

"Mr Tetley! Would you please lend us your axe?" asked Nick. "The one you chop wood with?"

"No, I will not!" exclaimed Mr Tetley. "I'll not lend you something to chop off your fingers!"

"Oh, Mr Tetley!" cried Laura. "We aren't as silly as that! Please do lend us the axe. It's for something secret and important, something we found in the woods."

"I suppose you want to chop up a dead tree," said Mr Tetley. "Listen now, I'll lend the axe to this young man, because he's the oldest and biggest, but no one is to use it except him, all right?"

"All right, Mr Tetley," said Katie and Laura. Nick took the axe, and they made their way out of the shed. But just as they turned towards the front gate, they heard Gran calling them.

"Bother!" said Laura. "It's lunch-time."

"Let's miss lunch and go and chop," said Katie, who was always ready to do mad things.

"Don't be silly," said Nick, putting the

axe carefully into the middle of the yew hedge to hide it. "We don't want to have Gran and Grandad hunting all over the place for us, and Mr Tetley telling them he's lent us the axe. No, we'll go in and have lunch, and then we'll spend the afternoon in the woods, chopping away the ivy and brambles!"

So they went in to lunch. There was a casserole, and treacle tart, and the three children ate hungrily. It was exciting to think of the axe hidden in the hedge, waiting to chop away creepers that had grown around a secret house.

"How you do gobble today!" said Grandad in astonishment. "Now, now, eat properly, or you'll be ill!"

"Gran, we found a pond in the middle of the woods this morning," said Laura, who could never keep quiet about anything.

"Did you?" said Gran. "Well, there used to be one, I believe. There was supposed to be a summerhouse there too, but it seems to have disappeared now. The stream has made the woods so marshy that it's not so nice to walk there as it used to be. Make sure you're careful if you go far into the woods as it gets very boggy."

"We'll put wellingtons on," said Nick. He frowned at Laura to stop her saying any more.

They slipped away from the dining-room as soon as they could. "I'm going to have a quiet nap," said Gran. "So keep away from the house, won't you?"

"Oh, yes, we'll be far away from Greylings this afternoon!" said Katie. She ran to join the other two. Nick was taking the axe from the hedge. It shone bright and sharp.

"Come on," he said. "We've got plenty of time now. We'll see what we can find!"

So off they went again with Russet, who was delighted to go hunting rabbits again. The children found the stream quite easily with Russet's help and followed its banks once more.

"Look! There's the pool!" said Laura, running towards it. "Come on! Do some chopping, Nick!"

CHAPTER 4

THE SECRET LITTLE HOUSE

Nick went to the overgrown clump and began to chop away at the ivy stems. He chopped hard above the steps where Russet had found a rabbit hole.

He hadn't chopped for long before he gave a shout. "Look! There *is* a house of some sort under all this ivy. I'm chopping by the door. Come and pull away the stems for me."

Katie and Laura went to help Nick. He had been chopping so furiously that his face was wet with perspiration. He took out his handkerchief and mopped his forehead.

The two girls began to tear away the broken stems of ivy. They were more careful with the blackberry sprays, because of the prickles. The honeysuckle came away easily, as its stems were thin and brittle.

"Yes!" said Katie excitedly. "There's a door behind here. Imagine there being a secret house hidden under all this ivy; a house forgotten for years and never used except by the rabbits."

Nick laughed. He took up his axe again. "Well, the rabbits must be getting a shock now," he said. "Stand away, you two. I don't want to chop your heads off!"

"Let me have a turn!" begged Katie, who was longing to chop too. But Nick shook his head firmly.

"Don't be silly, Katie," he said. "You know we promised that I'd be the only one to chop."

It was hard work. Some of the ivy stems were as thick as the trunks of small trees. The roots that these stems had put out held firmly to the door underneath, but once Nick had chopped the stems in half, it was easy to pull away the brown roots that clung everywhere.

"Nick, we've made quite a hole already!" said Laura in excitement. "Oh, Nick, hurry! Soon there will be enough room for us to creep through."

"Well, I'm hurrying as much as I can," said Nick. "But it's really tough going."

Crash! *Crash*! The axe cut through one

stem after another, and at last there was a
hole big enough to crawl through, round
the middle of the doorway. Nick twisted a
handkerchief round his hand and bent back
some of the prickly sprays that the others
couldn't manage.

He poked the axe through the hole. There was a wooden door behind. "I can see the handle!" said Nick.

He slipped his hand along the door and tried the handle but it wouldn't turn.

"I can't move it at all," he said.

"Let me try," said Katie. But she couldn't either, and nor could Laura. The handle was stiff with rust and wouldn't move. The three children were very disappointed.

"Let's see if we can find a window and chop the ivy away from that," said Laura. "Then we can get in through there."

So they tried to find a window but the creeping ivy and brambles were so thick that it was quite impossible to guess where a window might be. Scratched and pricked all over their arms, the children looked at one another and wondered what to do.

"There must be some way we can get in!" said Katie.

"Yes, there is!" cried Laura. "I know what to do!"

"What?" asked the other two.

"Chop down the door, of course!" shouted Laura excitedly. "Can't you chop a big enough hole in the door for us to squeeze through, Nick?"

"But do you think we ought to do that?" said Nick. "I mean, after all, it's a door, and it isn't right to chop holes in doors."

"It can't matter with this door," said Katie, eager to try Laura's idea. "It must be nearly falling to pieces as it is! Go on, Nick – chop a hole in it! We'll never get in if you don't. I can't wait any longer!"

Nick didn't want to wait either. He lifted the axe and chopped at the door with it. The wood was quite rotten and gave way easily. A few strokes, and there was a big hole in the door, through which the children could easily squeeze!

"Good!" said Nick, panting. "Hey! Doesn't it look dark in there?"

"I bet it's full of spiders and earwigs!" said Laura, staring at the dark hole in the door. "It's a good thing none of us is frightened of them. Who's going in first?"

Nobody seemed quite eager to go in after all! It did look decidedly dark and murky through the hole in the door. It smelled a bit funny too.

"I think I've got a torch here in my

pocket!" said Nick suddenly. He always carried a strange collection of things with him. He felt in first one pocket and then the other, and found a small torch.

"Oh, do hurry, Nick!" said Katie, always the impatient one. "I want to see inside this strange, secret house. I can't believe we've found it all hidden and covered with creepers, and nobody's been inside it for years and years!"

Nick switched on the torch, pointing it through the hole in the door. The three children crowded round to see inside the woodland house.

It looked very eerie in the torchlight. It was small, high and circular, and full of dark shadows. A bench ran round it, and there was a small fireplace at the back. A table stood against the wall at one side, with something on it. The children couldn't see what it was.

"Let's go in!" whispered Katie.

"What are you whispering for?" whispered back Laura.

"I don't know – but it seems wrong to speak out loud!" said Katie, still in a whisper.

Nick squeezed in through the hole first. "Oh! What's that?" he cried, and quickly climbed out again.

"What do you mean? What's the matter?" asked Laura, half frightened.

"Something touched my face," said Nick. "It was horrible!"

"It was a spider's web, you idiot," said Katie. She laughed, and the sound seemed to make things bright and ordinary again. "You baby, Nick! Imagine you being frightened of a spider's web!"

"Well, it felt pretty nasty stroking my cheek like that," said Nick. "You go in first, Katie, if you think a spider's web is so funny! Take the torch."

So Katie climbed in through the hole in the door, brushing aside the hanging spiders' webs with her hand. She shone the torch round the curious little house.

It had two windows, but both these were blocked up with ivy and other creepers. The bench round the wall was thick with the dust of many years. So was the table. Katie held the torch up and looked to see what was on it.

"Oh, the people who were here last drank

out of these glasses!" she said. "There are two here, all dirty and dusty. How weird to come here and find glasses still on the table!"

By this time the other two had crept into the little house too, and were staring round in excitement.

"Those glasses are like the old ones that Gran keeps in the drawing-room!" said Laura, picking one up. "She won't use them now because she says they are antique. How pleased she will be to have two more!"

"Look at the fireplace," said Katie, holding the torch up. "There's the remains of a fire there. What fun it must have been to come to this house on a cold day, light a fire, and sit here in the middle of the wood, with the lovely pool gleaming below!"

"Yes," said Nick. "I'd love a secret house like this. It's a shame it's gone to ruin."

"Well," said Laura. "This little house by the pool could be beautiful too. We could make it better. It's been hidden away and forgotten for years. Let's make it ours!"

"Oh, yes!" cried Katie and Nick, delighted with the idea.

"We'll clear away the ivy from the

windows and let the light through," said Laura, busy planning as she loved to do. "We'll clean up the whole house, and we'll make a fire here one day, and boil a kettle for tea!"

"Great idea!" shouted Nick, and he went to the door. A long spider's thread caught his ear and he rubbed it away. "I'd like to clear away these clinging cobwebs," he said. "I really don't like them!"

"Let's go home now," said Katie. "The torch battery is getting low so we can't do any clearing up now. We'll bring candles and matches when we come next time, and keep them on the mantelpiece."

"Let's take the two old glasses back with us," said Laura, picking them up. "Gran will be so surprised to see them!"

Off they went home, carrying the two glasses carefully. They whistled to Russet, who had been chasing rabbits, and then made their way through the dim woods. What an exciting day they had had!

CHAPTER 5

THE HOUSE HAS A SPRING-CLEAN

Gran and Grandad were amazed to hear about the secret house in the woods, but Gran was not at all pleased to hear of the axe.

"You're not to use such dangerous things," she said to Nick. "Mr Tetley was foolish to let you have an axe. You mustn't use that again."

"All right, Gran," said Nick. "But I'm really very careful, you know, and after all, I'm thirteen now."

"Look, Gran, here are the glasses," said Laura, putting them on the table. She had carefully washed them, and polished them with a clean cloth. They shone beautifully.

Gran gave a cry of delight and picked them up. "Look, Geoffrey!" she said to Grandad. "Two of those beautiful, heavy old glasses that we have in my cupboard over there. How lovely! These are rare now, children, and I am delighted to have them. They're over two hundred years old!"

She put them proudly in her glass-fronted cupboard in the corner of the drawing room. They were fat glasses, short and very heavy, and the children wished they could use them each day for their drinks but Gran wouldn't hear of it!

"Gran, we're going to make that little house our very own," said Laura. "We're going to clean it up, and keep a few books and things there. We'll scrub the steps that lead down to the pond and then, when it's all ready, you must come and have tea with us there!"

"We can make a fire and boil a kettle on the little hearth," Katie said happily. "There's a table there, and a bench round the wall. Oh, it's a very exciting place!"

"Well, I can't see why you shouldn't make it your own house if you want to," said Gran. "Greylings Wood is ours, and the house was ours too. So you can certainly have it for a playhouse, if you like."

They went to the house next day, and climbed in through the door again. This time they had plenty of candles and two candlesticks. They put two candles into the stands and stood them on the little mantelpiece. They lit the house well. Then Laura took charge of the cleaning.

"See what you can do about cleaning the windows," she said to Nick and Katie. "It'd be a good idea to let some light and air into the house. It still smells musty."

"We can't have the axe this time," said Nick, staring at the windows. "But I could borrow Mr Tetley's little saw, and saw through the ivy stems. It wouldn't take long."

So Nick ran back to Greylings and borrowed the saw. He and Katie took it in turns to saw the thick stems, and soon they were able to pull the ivy and brambles away from the windows, and let in the air and light. There was no glass in them, but it didn't matter.

Russet was delighted with the house. He jumped in and out of the hole in the door a dozen times an hour, and trotted all round the house, sniffing everywhere.

Nick and Katie did the clearing, while Laura tackled the cleaning. First she removed the cobwebs which stretched from wall to wall and hung down from the roof, grey with dust.

Next she swept down the walls with her broom. She brushed the mantelpiece, the bench, and the table. When she had got all the dust on to the floor, she began to sweep that into her pan. The dust made the children sneeze. They blew their noses, and then settled down to their work again. It was fun.

Katie fetched a bucket of water from the pond. The children had found that there was a complete flight of overgrown steps leading down from the little house to the pool. Katie was determined to uncover them and clean them all.

There was a lot to do, but the children enjoyed every minute. The sun was very hot in the garden of Greylings, but here in the woods it was cool and green. The children had brought lemonade with them, and they drank it when they felt too hot.

Laura scrubbed the floor, the bench, and the table. The floor was made of brightly-coloured tiles, set in a pattern, and at some time had had a rug over it, for Laura found threads of it left.

"Look! What a lovely floor!" said Nick, peering in through one of the window-holes. "It looks beautiful now! Who'd have thought there was a floor like that here!"

It took the children three days to get the little house really nice. At the end of that time it was unrecognisable.

Nick had managed to get the door to open and had cleared away all the creepers over the doorway, so that light came in there as well as in at the windows.

Katie had cleaned the steps that led down the pool. She had torn away the creeping roots that hid the gleaming marble, and had cleared them of earth and moss. She was very proud of them.

Laura had made the house look beautiful inside. Everything was spotless. The brightly-coloured tiles shone on the floor. The table and bench were quite clean, the fireplace was cleared too and was neatly laid ready for a fire, with paper, twigs and old wood that Nick had found outside.

They begged an old rug from Gran for the floor, and brought along a little vase which they filled with flowers for the middle of the table.

Laura even brought an old clock that she had found in a cupboard. It had belonged to Grandad, and one of its legs was broken.

Nick mended its leg. Laura wound it up and it went. So it stood on the mantelpiece, ticking away cheerfully!

"I think a clock makes a house feel cosy and lived in," said Laura. "Doesn't it all look nice? Let's have tea here tomorrow! We won't ask Gran and Grandad yet. We'll wait till we're sure the fire goes all right, and the chimney doesn't smoke."

The next day the children brought along the things for their first meal at the house. Laura carried a kettle of water so she could make tea. Nick brought a picnic basket full of food and Katie had a bag of unbreakable mugs and plates which Gran had given them for their house.

"Isn't this fun?" said Laura as she put a pretty cloth on the table. "Nick, do let me light the fire, please! After all, I did lay it ready." She knelt down and put a lighted match to the paper. It flared up at once, and the twigs began to crackle. The wood soon caught fire, and a lovely glow filled the hearth.

But it wasn't so lovely after a little while. Smoke began to pour out of the fireplace, and filled the little house. The children coughed.

"Oh no! It's smoking!" said Laura. "What a nuisance! Do you suppose we ought to have swept the chimney?"

"I wouldn't have thought the fire was used often enough to make the chimney really sooty," said Nick, "but maybe it's blocked with something."

Laura poked the lighted wood to the back of the fireplace, hoping that the smoke would soon go up the chimney. But it didn't. It went on pouring out into the room. Soon the children's eyes began to smart, and they choked with the stinging smoke.

"Wood smoke always does this," said Nick, going outside to wipe his streaming eyes. "We'll have to put the fire out, Laura. We can't boil water for tea today. We'll have to do that when we've put the chimney right."

"I expect it's stuffed up with ivy stems and leaves," said Katie. She kicked the fire out, and soon only a few wisps of smoke rose from the hearth. But it was impossible to have tea in the smoky house.

Laura was very disappointed. She took the food outside, and they sat on the steps, looking down to the little pond, and ate their egg sandwiches, ginger cake and chocolate biscuits there. They drank the water out of the kettle, pouring it into their mugs.

"This is an enchanted place!" said Katie. "Look how the sun comes slanting through the trees just there, and lights up the pond. What a lot of waterlilies there are today!"

"I could stay here all evening," said Laura. "But I'd really like to see what's the matter with that chimney, Nick. I want to put it right before Gran and Grandad come to tea!"

"Let's have a look at it now," said Nick, getting up. "Where's that brush you had yesterday? The one with a long handle, I mean. I could put that up the chimney to see if there's anything blocking it."

"It's over there," said Laura. "In the corner."

Nick took it. He went to the fireplace and knelt down beside it. "I expect there's a bird's-nest up there," he said. "It's a very short chimney, and it should be quite easy to clear."

He put the broom up and at once a shower of twigs and moss and leaves fell down into the fireplace. "There was a bird's-nest!" said Nick. He pushed the brush up again as high as it would go. "Katie, go outside and see if the brush is sticking out of the chimney," he said.

Katie went out and looked, then came back in again.

"Yes," she said. "I can just see it. The chimney should be clear now."

"Right," said Nick. He pulled the brush down, but the end of it stuck against something in the chimney. Nick tugged hard, but the brush-end wouldn't move.

"Bother!" he said. "What's the matter with it?" He put his arm up the chimney and felt about with his hand. To his surprise he found something jutting out halfway across. This was what the brush had caught on.

Nick felt round it. It seemed like a box, but made of metal, rather than wood.

"Come here!" he called. "There's an

opening in the side of this chimney, a kind of hidy-hole, I think! Something large has been stuffed into it and it's sticking out."

"Oh, Nick! Get it down! Quick, get it down!" shouted Katie and Laura.

"I'll try," said Nick, his face flushed with excitement. "It seems to have stuck. No, here it comes!"

CHAPTER 6

A Most Exciting Discovery

Nick had tugged so hard at the box that it had moved from its place. He slid it out from the hole. It was heavy and he couldn't hold it in one hand. The box fell down the chimney and landed in the back of the fireplace with a crash.

"Ugh!" said Katie. "What a dirty old box!"

"Isn't this exciting!" said Laura, hugging herself. "Could it be the treasure?"

"Don't be silly!" said Nick. "The box is much too small to hold the treasure! But it may hold something interesting, all the same."

It was an iron box, with a stiff clasp in front. On the top of the box was a raised letter – G. "G for Greylings," said Laura, tracing the letter with her finger. "This is an old Greyling box. Open it, Nick, quickly! Whatever can be inside?"

It wasn't easy to open. The years had made the clasp very stiff, and Nick took a knife from the picnic basket to force it open.

"Shake it, Laura, and see if it rattles," said Katie eagerly. "Perhaps it might have a few old brooches inside."

Laura shook it, but it didn't rattle.

"It sounds empty!" she said. "Oh, I do hope it isn't!"

Nick took the box from Laura and began to work at the stiff fastening. It suddenly gave way, and Nick opened the lid. The three children peered inside in excitement.

"There's nothing inside it at all!" said Nick in the greatest disappointment. "Look, it's quite empty!"

So it was. Nothing could be seen except the sides and bottom of the box itself.

Laura was puzzled. "But Nick," she said, "why should anyone want to hide a box in a secret chimney hole, if there was nothing in it?"

"How should I know?" said Nick gloomily. "It must have been hidden there years ago. A silly joke, perhaps."

"It couldn't have been a joke," said

Katie, taking the box from Nick. "Nobody sticks things up chimneys for a joke! Do you suppose there was something in the box, and somebody found it, then put the box back again after taking out the things inside?"

"Well, that's an idea," said Nick. "But how disappointing for us!"

Then Katie made a discovery. "Look," she said, holding up the box. "Doesn't it seem to you as if the box ought to be bigger inside than it is?"

"What do you mean?" asked the other two.

"Well," said Katie, "if you look at the outside of the box it seems quite big, but if you look inside, it doesn't look big enough!"

"You mean there might be a secret bottom to it?" cried Nick, and he snatched the box from Katie. He examined it very carefully and then nodded. "Yes, I think it does have a false bottom. You're right, Katie. How clever of you!"

"How can we open the secret part?" cried Laura, excitedly.

"I don't know," said Nick, busy pressing

and tapping to see if he could open it. "Hey! Suppose there is something extraordinary in here after all!"

Katie and Laura could hardly keep their hands off the box as Nick tried to open the bottom part. But it was no good, he couldn't do it. He gave it to Katie and she tried. Then Laura had a go. But no matter what they did they couldn't open it.

"It must be some sort of spring," said Nick in despair. "Oh, I do wish we could find it."

Laura grew impatient. She turned the box upside down and banged it with her fist. It slipped from her knee and fell on to the floor.

"Laura, be careful!" cried Nick, and then he stopped and stared at the box. It had fallen upside down, and the bottom of the box had slipped. Somehow or other in its fall the secret spring had been knocked, and the bottom was loose!

Nick grabbed the box and pressed on the bottom of it, holding it upside down. The bottom slid away neatly, and the three children saw a small narrow space inside, hidden between the false bottom and the

real one. And this time there was
something inside! It wasn't brooches or
anything like that – it was a sheet of thick
parchment folded over.

"Only a bit of paper," said Nick in
disappointment, taking it out very carefully.
It fell in two as he touched it, breaking at
the fold. It was obviously very old.

"What does it say?" asked Laura,
bending over to see it.

"It's a map," said Katie. "What a strange
old drawing!"

"So it is," said Nick. "But what's it a map of?"

"I've no idea," said Katie. "And what's this one word on the map just here? It's such old lettering that I can't even read it!"

"What's that first letter?" said Nick, trying to make it out. "It's a J, I think. J – and that's an R, I think. J – R – there's no word beginning with JR."

"J – R – and is that an E?" wondered Laura. "It's a funny one! And the next letter is certainly an A. Jrea – worse than ever!"

"And then comes an F," said Nick. "Jreaf – it must be some foreign language!"

"There are some more letters after that," said Katie. "I give up! But I know what we'll do. We'll ask someone who can read old writing, and see if they can tell us what the word is. Perhaps if we know what it is, we shall know what the map means."

"Oh no! Look at the time!" said Laura suddenly, staring at her watch. "Gran will be wondering what's happened to us! We'd better pack up and go home."

So they packed up their things, leaving the kettle behind for another day, and went home, carrying the old box with them.

As they came out of the woods they saw a car in the drive. "It's the same one that came the other day," said Nick, looking at it. "It belongs to those people who want to buy the house."

"Well, Gran and Grandad will be busy with them then," said Laura. "We'd better go into the study and wait till the visitors have gone."

So into the study they went and, of course, they got out the strange map, pieced it together once more, and tried to work out what the word said.

"If only we could find out!" sighed Laura.

And then a voice behind her said, "And what do you want to find out, my dear?"

The children looked round. They saw that Gran had come into the room with the tall man they had seen the other day, the man who wanted to buy the house. She was showing him the study once more, and the children hadn't heard the door open.

Nick did not want to say anything about the map. He tried to take it off the table but, as it was in two halves, he only managed to remove one piece before the man leaned over the table to look.

"I want to know what that word says," said Laura in her clear voice. "We've been puzzling and puzzling over it. It's an old map we found today, hidden in an iron box, up the chimney of our secret house in the woods."

Gran looked surprised. So did the man. He bent over the piece of parchment at once. "Where's the word?" he said. "Ah – well, let me see. That first letter is T."

"T! We thought it was a J," said Katie.

"T-R-E-A-S-" read the man.

"S!" said Katie scornfully. "That's not S, it's F."

"In the old days the letter S was written like an F," said the man. Then he jumped, because Nick gave a shout. He didn't mean to shout, but he couldn't help it. If the first letter was T – and the fifth was an S – then he knew what the word was!

But he didn't say it. He tried to take the paper out of the man's hand, but the man held on to it. "Wait, wait," he said, "I haven't finished. T-R-E-A-S-U-R-E. The word is treasure! How very interesting!"

The three children's faces went red with excitement and joy. "So it's a map showing where the treasure was hidden!" thought Nick to himself. "We can puzzle it out later and perhaps find the treasure for Gran!"

"May I take this old piece of paper to a friend of mine who is extremely clever at deciphering old papers?" said the man suddenly, turning politely to Gran. "I could perhaps find out a good deal more for you, Mrs Greyling, and it might be most interesting."

"Well, that's kind of you," said Gran, not knowing quite what to do. "But I'd rather like to keep the paper and show it to my husband."

"That's fine," said the man. "If I take it with me now and show it to my friend at once, I can send it back to you tonight with a note telling you what he says about it."

But Nick did not want the precious piece of paper to go out of his sight. "Please, it's ours," he said. "We want it. We found it ourselves."

"Of course, of course, my dear boy," said the man, smiling at Nick. "I quite understand your feelings. I'll only keep the paper an hour. My friend is staying at a hotel nearby, and will know at once whether it's genuinely old or not, and if it contains anything of importance to you. Your grandmother has been so kind to me that I would like to do her this little service, if I may."

Poor Gran could do nothing but smile and thank him. She did indeed think it was kind of him, but she was sorry because she guessed that the children wanted to show her their find and talk about it as soon as the man had gone. But as she hoped he would buy Greylings, she didn't want to offend him.

"Take it, by all means," said Gran politely. "It would be kind of you to find out exactly what the paper means, if it does mean anything!"

The man patted Nick on the shoulder. The boy was angry, and looked it. What right had this man to go off with their precious paper?

He went almost at once, carrying the parchment carefully in his hand.

The children clustered together as soon as Gran took the man out of the room.

"What did you want to go and tell our secret to a stranger for, you idiot?" said Nick, turning to Laura. "Now see what you've done! He's guessed it's something to do with the long-lost Greylings Treasure and he's taken the map. At least he's only got half of it! I was fast enough to grab the other half, and hide it behind my back before he saw it. So he won't be able to tell much from his half!"

"That was quick of you, Nick," said Katie. "But really, Laura, you were stupid to go and blurt out our secret like that."

"I'm sorry," said Laura, looking ready to cry. "I didn't think. I was so excited."

"If that's a map showing where the treasure was hidden, we don't want strangers going after it and finding it," said Nick. "You should have been quick enough to keep quiet."

"Don't go on at me so, Nick," said Laura. "I'm very, very sorry, really I am."

"Just keep your mouth shut another time," said Nick. "We'll have to wait and see what happens now. I only hope that man brings the paper back safely."

CHAPTER 7

MR POTS-OF-MONEY

Gran was told all about the finding of the box, and she called Grandad to hear about it when he came in. They looked at the old iron box with the big letter G on it. They exclaimed over the secret bottom, where the paper had been hidden. And Grandad longed for the man to bring back the parchment so that he could see the map himself.

"I shan't tell anyone that we've got the other half of the map," said Nick to the others, when they were alone once more. "Not anyone. This is our secret, and if there's going to be any finding of the treasure, we're going to do it, okay?"

The others agreed absolutely with Nick. They waited impatiently for the man to return.

"Supposing he doesn't?" said Laura. "Supposing he keeps the paper for himself and tries to get the treasure?"

"Oh, don't be silly, Laura," said Nick, who still felt cross with her. "How can he find anything if we've got one half of the map? Do use your brains."

"I am using them," said Laura indignantly. "He might be able to make out enough, just by using his half."

"Here he is again!" cried Katie from the window. "And he's got the map. Good!"

The man was shown into the study again, and Gran and Grandad came too, eager to hear what he had to say.

"I've taken the paper to my friend to decipher," said the man, whose name was Mr Potts. "He says there is no doubt at all that it is an old map, which shows the whereabouts of some treasure."

"Really?" said Gran, thrilled.

"Yes," said Mr Potts, his big moustache seeming to bristle with excitement too. "But my friend, who is used to dealing with old documents like this, says that there's only half of the real map here. He says there should be another half."

"Oh dear," said Gran, looking round the room as if she expected the other half to come floating down to her. "Now where can that be? In the box, do you think?"

"Quite likely," said the man eagerly. "May I look and see?"

Nick gave a secret wink at the others. He handed Mr Potts the box. He felt quite safe in doing so because he knew that there was nothing in it at all! The other half of the old map was in the top drawer of the desk in the corner. Nick had slipped it in there as soon as he had seen Mr Potts coming up the steps again.

Mr Potts shook the box. He opened and shut the false bottom. He peered into the secret hiding-place and scraped round it with a pencil. There was nothing there at all.

"No," he said. "It's quite empty. But I am perfectly certain there must be another half to this old map. Until it is found, no one will be able to hunt for the treasure. Do you know where it is?" he said very suddenly, wheeling round on Katie.

Katie had no idea where Nick had put the map. She shook her head. "No," she said, "I don't."

"Do you?" asked the man, staring at

Laura. Laura went very red. Like Katie, she had no idea where the other half was but she couldn't help blushing.

"I don't know where it is either," she said.

Mr Potts turned to ask Nick, but he had guessed he would be asked, and he had slipped out of the room. He wasn't going to tell a lie, but he wasn't going to tell the truth to Mr Potts either!

"I wonder if you children are telling the truth?" said Mr Potts, staring at the blushing Laura.

That made Gran angry. "Mr Potts," she said, "I think you forget that Laura is my granddaughter. Indeed, they are all truthful children, I can assure you."

"Sorry, Mrs Greyling," said the man, with a laugh. "This girl went so red I thought she might be concealing the truth."

"May we have our map back, please?" asked Katie, trying to make Mr Potts stop staring at Laura, who was looking more and more uncomfortable.

"Of course," said Mr Potts. "Here it is. But it isn't much use to you or to anybody unless the other half can be found."

He gave the map to Katie. "That word is certainly 'treasure'," he said. "And I should think that if we could find the other half of the map, and piece it together, there's a good chance of coming across the Greylings Treasure. You were good enough to tell me the old story the other day, Mrs Greyling, and I was most interested in it!"

"Well, thank you for your help," said Grandad.

"May I ask a favour?" said Mr Potts, smiling very charmingly at Grandad. "If you do come across the other half of the map, let me show it to my friend and he'll work it out for you, and help you to find the treasure. It needs someone very learned in old documents to decipher them, and I should be delighted to help you if I could."

"Thank you," said Grandad again. "We'll let you see the other half, if we find it."

"Where did you say you found the box?" asked Mr Potts, turning to Laura.

Laura told him, rather sulkily. She didn't want to tell him any more than she could help, after Nick's scolding, but if she didn't tell him, Gran would, so she didn't see that it mattered.

"Very interesting, very, very interesting," said Mr Potts, when he heard about the secret house, and the hole in the chimney. "You're very lucky children! Well, don't forget to let me know if you find the other half of the map, will you?"

He patted Laura on the shoulder, smiled at her sweetly, and then left the room with her grandparents. As soon as he was gone Laura stamped her foot.

"Horrible man! Patting me and smiling at me with a nasty treacly smile! He'd like to get the treasure himself, I know he would!"

"He's frightfully rich, Gran says," said Katie.

"Well, Potts is a good name for him then," said Nick, coming back into the room again. "Mr Pots-of-Money!"

The others laughed. "You were clever to slip out of the room before you could be asked if you knew where the other half was," said Katie. "Laura went awfully red. I thought Mr Pots-of-Money would guess that she knew about the other bit of map."

"Where's the half he brought?" asked Nick. Katie gave it to him. "Oh, great, now we'll be able to fit the pieces together and see what we can puzzle out. We may not be as clever and learned as Mr Potts's friend is, but I bet we're smart enough to see what this map means!"

"Let's go up to our room to look at it," said Katie. "If dear Mr Potts comes back suddenly, he might see we have two bits. And suppose Grandad sees them? He's promised to let Mr Potts have the other half if it turns up."

"Well, we mustn't let him or Gran know about the other half then," said Nick.

"Do come on. I'm dying to have a good look at the map again," said Katie.

"Let's go up by the secret staircase," said Nick. "Quick! Come into the dining-room before Gran or Grandad sees us and asks us about the missing bit of map."

They slipped unseen into the dining-room and went up the narrow stairs that wound up to Nick's room. All three children stepped out of Nick's cupboard, laughing.

"It's fun to come up those old stairs!" said Katie. "There's a table in our room, Nick. Let's go and spread out the map and really study it hard. Now that we know it's a map where the treasure was hidden, it's much more exciting!"

Soon the three children were bending over the mysterious old document. Nick carefully stuck the two halves together with sticky-tape so that they could see everything better.

"Look!" Katie said suddenly. "Do you see this half that Mr Potts took away? Compare it with the other half, and you'll see that every line on Mr Pott's piece looks dented, as if someone had run a pencil over them! Somebody has traced the map. So Mr Potts has got a copy of this! No wonder he was willing to bring it back so quickly!"

"That means he thinks it's a proper map, showing where the treasure is," said Laura slowly.

"It shows something else too," said Nick. "It shows that he means to try and find it! Why would he take a copy of it otherwise? No, he believes in the Greylings Treasure all right, and he believes in our map. How lucky he only saw half!"

"Do you think he may try to get the other half?" asked Laura solemnly.

"I hope not!" said Nick. "But you never know. I'm going to take a tracing of the map myself, and then put the real map into some good safe place so that we don't need to use it. We'll hide the tracing too, except when we need it."

"Do the copy now," said Katie. "I can see Gran and Grandad in the garden, and Mr Potts has gone. Then we can hide the real map away."

Nick got some tracing paper and sharpened a pencil.

In ten minutes he had carefully traced

the map on some paper, which he folded and put into his pocket.

"Now we'll hide the real map!" he said.

"Where?" asked Laura.

"It'd better be somewhere quite simple," said Nick. "Difficult places are always searched. I know! We'll put the map in your doll's-house – on the bedroom ceiling, and on the kitchen ceiling!"

He carefully stuck the two halves of the map on to the two ceilings in the doll's-house.

"Nobody would ever think of looking there!" said Laura in delight.

Then they heard Gran calling them for supper.

"Now we shan't have any time to work out the map!" said Nick. "Bother! We'll have to do it afterwards, when we come up to bed. We'd better wash now, and change into something clean. Hurry!"

CHAPTER 8

WHERE IS THE WINDING ROAD?

At supper that night Gran and Grandad asked the children all kinds of questions about the secret house and the iron box. They were really just as excited as the three children.

Nick said nothing at all about the other half of the map. Grandad wanted to see the piece that Mr Potts has borrowed and Nick took out his copy of it.

"I've put the map in a safe place," said the boy. "You see, Grandad, if people keep handling it, it will fall to pieces, it's so old!"

"Quite right, my boy," said Grandad, taking the tracing. "Very sensible of you."

The children went up early to bed that evening, for they all badly wanted to study the complete map and see if they could puzzle it out. As soon as Nick was undressed and had his dressing-gown on, he slipped into the girls' room.

They were already sitting at the table, studying the map. Nick joined them.

"It's an odd sort of map," said Nick. "Look at this curving snake thing, it must be a road! And then there are three big trees. Well, those trees may all be dead now and fallen down. But it's possible they're still standing in a row somewhere."

"And look at this funny hump-shape," said Katie, pointing with her finger. "Is it a hill? There aren't any hills like that round here, are there?"

"There might be," said Nick. "We haven't explored everywhere yet, and we don't know what's in the depths of that wood."

"Then there's this funny little drawing down here," said Laura, pointing to what looked like a sketch of a church. "It's got a row of odd little lines beneath it. Do you think they might show steps going up to it?"

"It's very difficult," said Nick, frowning as he tried to make out the map. "I read it like this: first we have to go down a winding road or lane; then we come somewhere where there are three big trees in a line; then we come to a hump-backed hill; near there we'll find a little church or building of some sort and perhaps the treasure is hidden nearby."

"That's brilliant, Nick!" said Laura, her eyes shining with excitement. "I wonder where the winding road is?"

"Let's look at a map of the district," said Nick. "It'll show us all the winding roads there are. We should come to the three big trees at the fourth bend in the road. If you count, you'll see there are four bends in the drawing."

"Yes, so there are," said Katie. "Oh, I'm longing to go exploring now. Where can we get a map to see if there are any winding roads round here?"

"I believe there's one in Grandad's study," said Laura. "I saw Grandad looking at it the other day. Shall I slip down and fetch it?"

"Yes," said Nick. "Go down the hidden staircase, Laura. You won't be seen then."

Laura ran into Nick's room, opened his cupboard door, and went down the curious little stairs. She stopped at the bottom to listen in case there was anyone in the dining-room. She could hear nothing. She stepped into the dining-room, ran to the door and then crept into the study. She could hear the television murmuring in the drawing-room.

"Good!" thought Laura. "If I do make a bit of a noise, no one will hear me with the TV on!"

She opened the glass front of the bookcase. It made a click as it opened but nobody heard. Laura hurriedly looked down the row of books. She was sure the map had been put back there. Yes, there it was: "Map of Greylings Land".

She took it out of the bookcase, shut the glass front, which made an alarming click again, and then ran back to the staircase. She was up it and into Nick's bedroom in seconds.

"Great!" said Nick, pleased, when Laura rushed in holding the map. "You've been very quick, but what a row you made! We heard the click of the bookcase up here!"

"I couldn't help it," said Laura. "But the TV's on, so Gran didn't hear anything. Come on, let's see if we can find this winding road."

They opened the big folded map. It showed all the land held by the Greyling family. There were the two farms, the manor house and its grounds, Greylings Wood, and the roads around and through the property.

"It's huge," said Nick. "I hate to think of it all going to Mr Pots-of-Money. He's not the right person to have it. I bet he'll turn the people off the farms and cut down all that lovely wood to sell for timber!"

"Look. Would you call that a winding road?" asked Katie, pointing to a place called Cuckoo Lane.

"It's not very winding," said Nick. "And it only seems to have three bends, not four. Let's see if there's a road that winds more than that."

They studied the Greylings map from end to end. They looked at every road, and every lane. They even studied the field paths that were shown running here and there.

"Right then, Cuckoo Lane seems to be the only road or lane that winds at all," said Nick at last. "Maybe we'll find that it has more bends than the map shows. The other roads are either straight, or just sort of wavy with no proper bends."

"It's very flat ground round here," said Laura. "People can walk straight from place to place. It's where there are hills that roads wind a bit."

"What shall we do tomorrow?" asked Katie, folding up the big map. "Shall we go to Cuckoo Lane and see if we can find four bends in it, and maybe three enormous trees and a hill somewhere?"

"Yes, good idea," said Nick. "We'll go tomorrow morning, and in the afternoon we'll ask Gran and Grandad to have tea at the secret house with us. That'll be fun!"

There was the sound of someone coming up the stairs to the landing outside. "Quick, Nick, it's Gran!" whispered Laura. "Get back to your room!"

Nick shot across the room, slipped into his bedroom and jumped into bed as Gran opened the girls' door.

"I heard you talking, my dears," said Gran. "It's quite time you put out your light and went to sleep. You'll wake Nick if you talk like this."

Katie giggled. She knew quite well that

she wouldn't wake Nick, who was wide awake already! She and Laura snuggled down under the bedclothes. Gran bent over and kissed them both goodnight.

Then she tiptoed into Nick's room, and straightened his quilt. Nick didn't make a sound. But you should have heard those three children giggling as soon as Gran went downstairs!

"Nick, I hope we don't keep you awake with our talking!" called Katie.

"Be quiet, Katie," said Nick, "or you'll have Gran back again! We'd better sleep now and dream of the winding lane leading to the treasure!"

CHAPTER 9

A VISIT TO THE TAYLORS' FARM

The next day the children asked Gran and Grandad if they would come to tea at the little house.

"Yes, we'd love to," said Gran. "We're longing to see it! We'll all have tea there at four. What are you going to do this morning?"

"We're going for a walk, Gran," said Nick. "Unless you want us to do anything for you?"

"No," said Gran. "It would be nice for you to go out. Where are you going?"

"Along Cuckoo Lane, I think," said Nick. "Though I don't know whether Russet can walk after such a huge breakfast!"

"You shouldn't feed him at mealtimes," said Gran. "He gets so many scraps that he'll grow quite fat. Won't you, Russet?"

"Woof!" said Russet, leaping about the

room excitedly, having heard the wonderful word "walk"!

"You'll pass near the Taylors' house," said Grandad, looking up from his paper. "Go in and say hello to Mrs Taylor. She'll be delighted to see you."

The children set off as soon after breakfast as they could. Russet pranced ahead of them, barking at the sparrows on the path. Nick had with him the copy of the map.

They went down the drive and out through the gates. The stone eagles sat on the gateposts, looking over the road as they had done for four hundred years. They were so old that they had begun to crumble away.

Down the road went the children, followed by Russet, till they came to a stile. They climbed over it into a large field. There was another stile at the other end, and then a narrow path that ran between two tall hedges.

"We come into Cuckoo Lane at the end of this path," said Nick, looking at the big map. "It looks as if Cuckoo Lane begins at two cottages and then wanders across a common to Mr Taylor's house."

The children walked along the narrow path. "Cuckoo Lane starts here," cried Katie, reaching the cottage gates. "We'll follow it carefully and count the bends."

They set off down the lane. On one side was a low hedge of hawthorn. On the other there was nothing except the common stretching away, soft and heathery.

"Here's one bend," said Laura, as they rounded a corner. "Good! But the lane looks awfully straight now, doesn't it? It looks straight almost as far as Mr Taylor's house."

"Well, it might go past his house after all," said Nick, "or there may be a few bends we can't see."

Down the lane they went, curving round a duck-pond that Nick thought they might call another bend. Then, as it came to the Taylors' house, the lane wound round to his front gate.

"That's three bends, anyway," said Katie, pleased. "Nick, let's just see if the path goes on, before we call on Mrs Taylor."

But, to their great disappointment, it seemed to stop at the farm gate. Only field paths were to be seen after that.

"Isn't that frustrating!" said Katie. "Maybe the old map is wrong. Perhaps there should have been only three bends shown?"

"Could be," said Nick. "But what I'd like to see is some big trees. There's too much common round here, and I can't see any big tree except that one over there by the farmhouse."

"And where's the hill?" asked Laura, looking all round. "The land is so flat here. I can't see a hill even in the distance!"

"It's very disappointing," said Nick. "Let's go in and see if Mrs Taylor is anywhere about. She may be able to tell us if the lane ever went any farther than this. After all, this map is very old, and lanes can disappear easily enough if they are not used."

They went into the farmyard. Cows mooed in a shed nearby. Pigs grunted in a big sty. Hens clucked in every corner, and from somewhere came the curious sound of turkeys gobbling.

"There's Mrs Taylor with the turkeys!" said Laura. "Hello, Mrs Taylor! We've all come to see you!"

Mrs Taylor shut the door of the turkey-house. She beamed at the three children, who liked her at once. She was plump and smiling, and her face shone like a large, red, polished apple.

"Well, I never!" she said. "Laura Greyling and two friends. Welcome, my dears, I'm right glad to see you all! This must be Nick and this must be Katie. We heard you were living with Laura and I'm happy to meet you both. I was wondering when I'd get a sight of your pretty face, Laura. How like your father you are! Ah, I remember him here as a boy, and what a monkey he was too! Let all my turkeys out one day, he did, and such a time we had getting them back."

"Did Dad really do that?" said Laura in the greatest surprise. She couldn't imagine her father doing anything so naughty. "Oh, I must ask him about it!"

"Yes, you ask him if he remembers Mrs Taylor's turkeys!" said the farmer's wife, with a laugh. "It was this very house he let them out of, the rascal! But come along, we don't want to stand here talking about my greedy turkeys! You come in and I'll see if I can find a few cakes for you, and something to drink!"

They followed her into the sunny farmhouse. They sat down in a huge kitchen, the floor of which was tiled with old red bricks, so clean that it seemed a shame to tread on them. At one end burned a cheerful wood fire. Bright red geraniums flowered on the windowsill, and cups and saucers with a bright red pattern seemed to flower on the dresser.

"It's a lovely kitchen," said Laura, looking round. "When I'm grown up I'll have a kitchen like this."

Mrs Taylor disappeared into a larder as big as Grandad's study. She brought out chocolate buns, some tarts that were so full of home-made jam that they ran over, and a great jug of something that looked a little like lemonade, but wasn't.

"It's nettle beer, my dears," said Mrs Taylor. "Nettle lemonade! Made of the youngest leaves of the hedgerow nettles, according to an old recipe that my great-grandmother had from Greylings Manor when she was a cook there a hundred years ago!"

The children tasted the nettle drink and thought it was delicious. They ate all the buns and the tarts and were very sorry when they were finished. They were too polite to ask for any more. Russet sat beside them, licking up any crumbs that were dropped!

"I'll not give you more to eat," said Mrs Taylor, who knew quite well what the children were thinking. "I've plenty to offer you, but I know you'll not be eating any lunch if you have too much now! And what will your grandmother say to me then?"

The children laughed. They loved being in the old kitchen and having such a feast.

"Is the farmhouse very old?" asked Katie, looking up at the enormous black beams that ran across the ceiling of the kitchen.

"Oh, yes," said Mrs Taylor. "As old as Greylings Manor. Ah, Laura, I'm grieved to hear that your grandparents are leaving. We've belonged to Greylings, we Taylors, as long as anyone knows. We don't want to belong to strangers!"

"Isn't it a pity that the Greylings Treasure can't be found?" said Laura.

"Then Grandad would be rich."

"The Greylings Treasure has been lost for many years," said Mrs Taylor, gathering up the dirty plates. "Many a man has hunted for that, my dears. But it's my belief it went years and years ago. It'll never be found now."

"Is the lane old that comes to your house, Mrs Taylor?" asked Nick.

"As old as the house, I guess," said the farmer's wife.

"Did it ever go further than the house?" asked Nick.

"No, never," said Mrs Taylor. "It had no need to. There's no house beyond this one. It only runs between the two cottages down the way and our farm."

The children were disappointed to hear that. But they didn't tell Mrs Taylor why they wanted to know. They went outside to see the young chicks and ducklings at the back of the farm, and to look at the lambs frisking in the fields beyond.

"What's that old place over there?" asked Katie, pointing to a tumbledown stone hut with no roof, not far off. Lambs were playing in and out of it.

"No one knows," said Mrs Taylor. "It's been like that for years. I did hear say that there was something funny about it, but I never found out what. There's not much left of it now."

"Let's go and look at it," said Laura.

But there wasn't time. "No, we must hurry back," said Nick. "We've been away all morning! Russet, Russet! Stop sniffing about, and come along home!"

They said goodbye to Mrs Taylor, who begged them to come again soon. They hurried down the lane, counting the bends again.

"It's no good, there are only three," said Nick. "And one of those isn't much of a bend really. Nor are there any big trees about, and I didn't see a hill at all, did you? I looked everywhere when we went round the farm."

"So did I," said Katie, looking gloomy. "I'm afraid this lane can't be the right one. We'll just have to think again, that's all!"

CHAPTER 10

SOMEONE ELSE IS TREASURE HUNTING!

That afternoon the children and their grandparents went to picnic in the little house.

Gran didn't like the marshy ground she had to cross at all, so Nick kept putting down handfuls of twigs on the muddiest bits for her to walk on.

Russet came with them, of course, quite beside himself with joy at chasing the rabbits again. His tail wagged the whole time, and his tongue hung out of his mouth.

"We'll make a fire again this afternoon," said Laura happily. She loved making fires. "I hope the chimney won't smoke this time."

"It shouldn't smoke now," said Nick. "It was the bird's-nest and the iron box that made it smoke, because they were blocking the chimney."

Gran and Grandad were amazed when they saw the secret house, and looked at the doorway and windows which the children had cleared by chopping and sawing away the ivy and brambles.

"I had heard of this place," said Grandad. "But even when I was a boy it had disappeared. I remember looking for it, and thinking it must have fallen to pieces. It must have been overgrown even then, and I didn't see it."

Laura went to lay the fire. She stopped and stared in surprise. The fireplace was not as she had left it. It had been full of twigs and leaves and moss. But now it wasn't! The mess had been cleared out of the fireplace, and was over the floor.

"Look," said Laura to Nick, "somebody has been here!"

Nick stared at the fireplace. He remembered that they hadn't stopped to clear it out after finding the box up the chimney. How strange!

"Why should all that mess have been moved away from the hearth?" wondered Nick. "I know! There can only be one reason!"

"What?" asked Laura.

"Because somebody was hunting around for something!" said Nick. "Somebody has been looking for the other half of the map! Yes, that's what has happened. They've looked up the chimney and cleared the hearth to hunt for it, too. And look! They've caught their sleeve on this old nail!"

The nail stuck out from the mantelpiece and on it hung a small piece of blue cloth.

"Mr Potts wore a blue suit yesterday," said Laura. "I bet he's been here hunting and torn his suit. Serve him right!"

"Well, he didn't find much!" said Nick. "I wish I'd caught him."

"I don't," said Laura. "He would be rather unpleasant. I don't like him!"

Laura didn't tell her grandparents what they had discovered. They quickly cleared away the mess, and Laura laid and lit a fire in the hearth. This time it burned beautifully and didn't smoke at all. The children were very pleased. Katie put the kettle on the fire to boil.

They had a lovely picnic, except that Russet discovered the chocolate buns, which Katie had stupidly put on the floor for a moment. He quite thought the plate was meant for him, and he ate six of them before he was noticed! Then he was driven out of the house in disgrace, and spent his time pawing in the pool at a big fish he could see under the water.

"I know he'll fall in," said Laura. But he didn't. He wasn't fond enough of water for that!

"Well," said Gran, when the picnic was over, "that was a real treat. I think you've cleaned the house beautifully, Laura darling. The three of you will be able to have it as your own hidy-hole while you are at Greylings."

"The pool is very pretty from here," said Grandad, sitting on a step and looking down at the lilies. "I like that bit of the stream you see too. It winds in and out beautifully between the trees."

"Yes, doesn't it?" said Katie. Then a thought struck her. It was such a wonderful thought that she went red at once. She beckoned to Nick and took him behind the little house. He was puzzled by her excited face.

"Nick! Did you hear what Grandad said?" whispered Katie.

"Of course," said Nick. "But what about it?"

"Nick, when he said the stream winds in and out beautifully, didn't you think of anything!" cried Katie, forgetting to whisper. "Don't you see? We've been looking for a winding lane, but it's a stream on the map, not a lane!"

"Hey! You're right!" said Nick. "Yes, why didn't we think of that before? The stream, of course, and its fourth bend. Wow! We'll have some more exploring to do tomorrow!"

They told Laura, who had just come up to see what the excitement was. She glowed with delight. "Of course!" she said. "We are idiots not to have thought of that. Good old Grandad! He gave us the clue to the mystery and didn't know it!"

Gran wondered why the children seemed so excited when they went home that evening. But they didn't say a word! No, this was their own secret, and they meant to do their exploring without anyone knowing.

"Now somebody else is doing a bit of exploring too, we'll keep our secret all the closer!" said Nick, remembering the fireplace in the little house. "Mr Potts has been to our house, but he doesn't know any more than he did before!"

"Well," said Gran, when they reached home, "that was a lovely outing. You were clever to discover that hidden house, children, it really is exciting. I can imagine how thrilled you were to find the iron box in the chimney too, and the old map. It's a great pity that there is only one half of it."

"Well, the other half may turn up," said Grandad. "If so, we'll let that fellow Potts have it and see if his clever friend can make out what it means, though I'm afraid it probably doesn't mean anything."

The children looked at one another, but they said nothing. Laura longed to tell everything, but she knew she mustn't.

They went up to their rooms, and Katie made an odd discovery! She opened one of her drawers to get a clean handkerchief and, to her great surprise, she found that the drawer was very untidy!

"Which of you has been untidying my

drawers?" she shouted to Laura and Nick. "I only tidied them this morning. Gran scolded me yesterday because they were untidy, so I spent ages folding everything neatly and now they're all higgledy-piggledy again."

Laura opened her drawers too, and found they were not as neat as she had left them. She was as puzzled as Katie.

Nick went to his room and pulled out his drawers one by one. He called to the others: "Mine are the same! Someone has been through them as well. This is very peculiar!"

The girls came into Nick's room and they all looked at one another. They each thought the same thing.

"It's Mr Potts, or somebody to do with him," said Laura slowly. "They've been looking for the other half of the map. They've guessed we've got it, because I went so red yesterday when they questioned me about it."

"So they came and hunted through our things while we were out," said Nick. "The burglars!"

"Nick! You don't think they've found the

halves of the map, do you?" said Katie suddenly.

"Oh, I hope not!" said Nick. He rushed to the doll's-house and knelt down. He switched on the little electric lamps that lit the house and looked inside. He gave a sigh of relief.

"No, it's all right," he said. "They're

here, safe on the ceilings. It's lucky we thought of such a good hiding place!"

"Let's go downstairs and find out if Mr Potts called," said Katie. In the hall they found Jane, the housekeeper, arranging some flowers.

"Hello, Jane," said Laura. "Did anyone call while we were out this afternoon?"

"Yes, Laura. Mr Potts came, and another gentleman," said Jane. "They said they would like to see you children. They were sorry you were out."

"Did they come into the house?" asked Nick. "Or did they go off straight away in their car?"

"Mr Potts asked if his friend might use the telephone," said Jane. "So I showed Mr Potts into the dining-room and took his friend to the hall telephone. He was there nearly fifteen minutes!"

"Was Mr Potts waiting in the dining-room all that time?" asked Nick.

"I expect so," said Jane.

The children ran off. "I bet he didn't wait in the dining-room all that time!" said Katie. "He slipped up the little staircase to Nick's room and had a good hunt round while his friend was pretending to telephone. He's clever, is Mr Potts!"

"Nick, I don't think you ought to carry the map tracing about with you," said Laura anxiously. "Suppose he caught you and searched you. He'd find it!"

"You're right, Laura," said Nick. "Hey, I know a way to trick dear Mr Potts! I'll make a false map and keep it in my pocket! Then, if he does catch me and search for the map, and find it, he'll be on the wrong track because the one he'll be following is a false one!"

"That's clever, Nick," said Laura. "You'd better do it tonight and we'll burn the tracing you made, after learning it by heart! We can always turn the doll's-house upside down and study the map on the ceilings if we forget anything!"

So that night Nick made a false map. At least, half of it was quite correct, because Mr Potts had seen the half with the words "treasure" on it, but the other half was a real muddle!

Nick drew four more bends in the stream instead of two. He drew six more trees, a few small bushes, and then something that looked like a piece of bread-and-butter with a bite out of it!

"Whatever's that?" asked Katie in surprise.

"I don't know!" said Nick, with a laugh. "Just something to puzzle Mr Potts, that's all!"

He burned the other tracing, after the three of them had studied it very carefully, and knew it so well that each of them could draw it correctly from memory. Then Nick slipped the false map into his pocket.

"Now Mr Potts can find it if he likes!" he said.

"Nick, let's go and find the four bends in the stream tomorrow," said Katie. "I'm longing to do some more exploring."

"Right!" said Nick. "We'll go treasure hunting again for all we're worth!"

CHAPTER 11

THE CHILDREN FOLLOW THE MAP

The next day the three children set off once more with Russet. They had wanted to take a picnic lunch but Gran had said no.

"Mr and Mrs Potts have kindly asked you all to tea this afternoon," she said. "I'll take you in the car but I want you home for lunch so that you can tidy yourselves and change into something nice afterwards."

"Oh, what a nuisance!" said Laura. "I don't like Mr Potts."

"Well, perhaps you'll like his house and grounds," said Gran. "He has a wonderful lake, so he tells me, and four boats. He says you can go out in one."

"Oh, good," said Katie, who loved boating. "That won't be so bad."

"All the same, it's a waste of time when we have so much exploring to do," said Nick, as they got ready to go to Greylings Wood.

Russet knew the way to the secret house very well now and set off on the usual path at once. But Nick called him back. "Hi, Russet! We're not going that way today!"

"Which way are we going then?" asked Laura, surprised.

"We want to find out where the stream enters the woods," said Nick. "I think we must count the bends from where the trees begin. I asked Mr Tetley and he said we had to go down the road for about a mile, then we'd see the stream flowing under a bridge."

So Russet and the children went down the road in the sunshine. After about twenty minutes' walk, they came to a small stone bridge that spanned the stream.

"Here it is," said Nick. "Come on, we'll leave the road here and go into the woods."

There was no hedge, and no railing. The children simply walked among the trees and followed the stream. It ran quite straight for a little way and then curved slightly.

"Is this one of the bends, do you think?" asked Laura excitedly.

Nick shook his head. "No," he said. "We

must look for fairly big bends, I think. They were very curved on the map."

A pleasant path ran by the bank of the stream for some way. Then the path stopped at an old wooden seat, and the children had to scramble along through an overgrown part of the wood for some time.

Just after the wooden seat the stream took a great turn to the left, almost doubling over on itself.

"The first bend!" said Nick, pleased. They followed the curve as best they could, and almost at once the stream curved again, this time to the right.

"The second bend!" said Katie. "We're getting on!"

They were in a part of the woods that they didn't know but, after they had followed the stream for a little while longer, they suddenly came to the part that led to the pond by their secret house!

Laura was surprised. The other two laughed at her. "But Laura, you must have known that we would come to it some time," said Nick. "After all, it's the same stream!"

"Yes, I know," said Laura. "But I just

didn't think we'd arrive here somehow. Look, there's a fine bend just beyond the pond, so that's the third one!"

They scrambled round the pond, and tried to follow the third bend. But it was quite impossible because the ground was so marshy that they sank almost up to their knees. Russet hated it. He stood and barked loudly at the children.

"He thinks we're quite mad!" said Katie. "Come on, Russet! Don't get left behind."

Russet ran off round the trees.

"We'd better follow him," said Nick, pulling his foot out of a muddy hole. "We can't possibly go this way. We'll come to the stream again after skirting this marshy bit."

So they followed Russet between the trees on drier ground. He seemed to know that they didn't want to go very far from the water for as soon as possible he led them back to it.

Nick stood on the bank and looked back up the stream, the way they had come. It was almost straight after the third big curve.

"Only one more bend, and then we should come to the three large trees or the humpy hill," said Nick. "Come on. It's drier here."

They were able to follow the stream better now. Great beeches grew all around, and the undergrowth was scarce. Some of the beech trees were so old and knotted that they seemed to have strange faces in their wrinkles.

At last the children came to the fourth bend. This was a good one. The stream swung round to the right and then the children saw before them a magnificent avenue of trees, planted in two straight rows, with what must once have been a grassy lane between them.

The space between them was no longer a lane but was completely overgrown with bushes and undergrowth of all kinds. But it was easy to see what a fine avenue it must have been, for the trees still stood there, swaying in two long rows.

"Somebody must have planted this avenue," said Nick. "Perhaps they liked to ride here, or maybe it was a proper road at one time, leading to somewhere."

"The only problem is – where are our three big trees?" said Laura. "With so many trees it's difficult to know which are the right three!"

Nick stared at the trees. He noticed that they were not as big as some of the others they had passed on their way through the woods.

"I don't think these trees are more than a hundred years old," he said at last. "So they couldn't have been planted at the time that map was drawn. It's three times bigger, much older trees we must look for, more like those enormous old beeches we passed a little way back."

"Do you think it might be three of those that we want?" said Laura.

"Of course not," said Nick. "We want three trees after the fourth bend in the stream, not before. Let's hunt about the place for three enormous old trees. I only hope they haven't died or been cut down."

They made their way through the trees, looking for three together. Laura came across a great old tree, with such a thick, knotted trunk that she felt sure that the tree must be hundreds of years old.

"Here's a very old tree," she called. "It's huge! Oh, there's another not far off.

They're two of the oldest trees we've seen."

"Where's the third?" said Nick, looking around. "These two are certainly enormous. Oh, look, Katie, look, Laura, there's the stump of a third old tree! In between these two we've found, do you see? There were three trees here once, but one must have died and been cut down. Lucky its stump was left to show us where it grew!"

The children stared at the two gnarled old giants and the stump of the third. They were in a slanting line, just as the map had shown.

"There are no other trees in a diagonal as far as I can see," said Nick, hunting around. "They are either in straight lines, like those in the avenue, or they are just growing anywhere. These must be the three!"

"Well, now we must look for the humpy hill," said Katie. "How will these trees help us? Do we have to follow the direction in which they are pointing?"

"Either that, or we climb one of the trees and see what we can find!" said Nick.

"Climb up the biggest one!" said Laura.

"I'll climb this one and you climb that one," said Katie to Nick. So each climbed up one of the old trees. They had to be careful because the twigs were brittle, and some of the boughs were quite dead.

At last they got to the top. And then Nick gave a shout. "I can see something!"

"What?" shouted Laura at the bottom.

"A humpy hill!" cried Nick.

"Oooh!" said Laura, almost beside herself with excitement. "Where is it?"

"In the very thickest part of the woods, I should think!" said Nick. "Wait a minute, I've got my compass. I'll set it so that I know exactly which direction the hill is."

Katie could see nothing because her view towards the hill was hidden by Nick's enormous tree. She climbed down quickly. Nick climbed down too, slipping on one bough and grazing his knee rather badly. But he was too excited to do any more than mop his knee with his handkerchief.

"It's odd," he said. "The hill sticks up just above the top of the trees yet there are no trees on it at all, as far as I could see. It's just covered in grass. It's buried so deep in the woods that no one would ever find it unless they knew it was there. Oh I say, aren't we getting on!"

He showed the others his compass. "I've got to keep the needle pointing exactly there," he said, showing them the little swinging needle in its round glass case. "If I do, and we follow that direction, we're bound to come to the humpy hill. Wow, isn't this exciting!"

They set off in the direction the needle pointed – due north. It was difficult going, for the wood was very dense indeed, and the children had to force their way through. The beech trees had given way to oak, hazel and birch and undergrowth, untrimmed for years, had grown thick and matted.

Soon their arms were scratched and their clothes were torn. But they couldn't stop. It was far too exciting!

After forcing their way through the woods for about twenty minutes they came suddenly to the hill. It rose very steeply from the floor of the wood, covered with grass and bracken.

"Great! That's the hill!" said Nick in delight. "We *are* reading the map well!"

CHAPTER 12

RUSSET IS A GREAT HELP!

The three children looked at the strange humpy hill. A rabbit peeped out of a burrow and popped back. Russet was up the hill like a flash of lightning and put his head down the hole.

"Shall we climb the hill?" asked Katie.

"Well, we'll be awfully late for lunch," said Nick, looking at his watch. "But we must go on a bit further and see if we can find that church-like place!"

So they climbed up the hill, seeing little rabbit paths here and there. When they got to the top they were amazed. They were level with the treetops and could look over the canopy of the wood, seeing the swaying branches for miles! It was a lovely sight.

They couldn't see any sign of a little church, though. They looked on all sides of the hill but there was no building of any kind. It was really disappointing.

"I hope we're not going to lose the trail just as we've followed the map so well," said Nick. "But I can't see any building. Can you, Katie?"

"No, I can't," said Katie gloomily. "Let's go down the other side of the hill and hunt around a bit. Perhaps the church was built among the trees and is hidden from us."

So down the other side of the steep, humpy hill they went, and hunted around to see what they could find, but they found nothing at all.

It was Russet who discovered something! He shot after a rabbit that had ventured too near him, and when it dodged under a bush, he rushed after it and began to scrape away the earth there. Nick pulled him out, and then called to the others.

"Come and look here. Russet has uncovered part of a big stone, as grey as Greylings' gateposts!"

They crowded round to look. They scraped away more of the moss and creeper, and sure enough, it was an old chiselled stone.

"I guess it was once part of a wall," said Nick. "We are stupid! That old building shown on the map must have fallen down ages ago! All we'll find will be the great blocks of stone, like this one, that it was built of. Let's look."

They began to hunt, scraping away moss here and there, and pulling away brambles, until at last they found enough stones to show where some building had been. It wasn't a large building, from the rough outline of its shape revealed by the stones the children had unearthed.

"Well, this was the building all right," said Laura. "The thing is, where are the steps that led up to it? You remember the lines that looked like steps in the picture, don't you?"

They remembered quite well. "I don't see how there could possibly have been any steps to this building," said Katie, puzzled. "It's built flat on the ground. If it had been built on the hill, there might have been steps leading up to it, as there are to our secret house from the pond, but you can't have a flight of steps if you build on the ground itself!"

Nick was puzzled and disappointed. It was too bad that they had found everything except the steps! He looked at his watch and gave a shout. "Help! It's one o'clock already and lunch is at one. We will be in trouble! Come on, we must go at once. We'll come back tomorrow."

"Isn't there a shorter way home?" asked Katie, thinking with dismay of the thick wood they would have to force their way through again.

"Well, if there is, we don't know it!" said Nick. "Hi, Russet! Where are you going? Come back!"

Russet was trotting off in another direction. He took no notice of Nick at all.

"Russet!" yelled Nick angrily. "Don't pretend to be deaf. Come here! You'll be lost if you go wandering off by yourself when we're so far from home!"

Russet stopped and looked back at them. He cocked his ears up, and put on a most cheeky expression. But he didn't come back.

So Nick ran after Russet who at once began trotting off again in the opposite direction. It was most annoying. Everyone called and shouted, and ran after the little dog, but he still wouldn't come.

Then Laura noticed that Russet really did seem to know the way he was going. She stopped for a moment. "I think Russet knows another way!" she said thoughtfully. "After all, he can find his way home from anywhere in Faldham Wood. Shall we follow him?"

"Yes," said Katie. So all three children followed Russet, who wagged his tail, very pleased. He led them through the woods, leaving behind the very thick part and then, most unexpectedly, came out at the field behind Mr Taylor's house!

"Wow!" said Nick, amazed. "Who would

have thought we were so near the farm? That's really lucky. Now we can run home all the way from here, instead of scrambling through the woods. It will be a shorter way to come tomorrow too."

They set off home at a trot, and arrived at a quarter to two, dirty, tired, hungry and with their clothes torn and arms and legs scratched. Gran was very cross indeed.

"You naughty children!" she said, coming out of the dining-room and catching them just as they were creeping upstairs to wash and change. "Three-quarters of an hour late! You don't deserve any lunch at all! Just look at your clothes, and what have you done to your knee, Nick?"

"Oh, nothing much, Gran," said Nick, looking down at his badly-grazed knee which he had forgotten about. "I climbed a tree and slipped as I was climbing down again. Really, it's nothing."

"I'll give you five minutes to wash and put on something clean," said Gran. "If you are not down by then I'll take the lunch away and you can have bread and cheese instead."

They all shot upstairs, and soon taps were running and clothes were being hurriedly changed. They rushed into the dining-room just in time!

"Now I don't want you to speak a word," said Gran, still cross with them. "Eat your lunch, and try to make up for your bad behaviour."

So they ate hungrily, and didn't say a word. Grandad had had his lunch and was in the garden, reading.

"You must be ready at three o'clock to go with me in the car to Mr Potts's house," said Gran, when they had finished. "It's nearly half past two now. Wash again, a little more carefully, and I'll find a plaster for that awful knee, Nick. Do your hair properly, put on your best things, and be down in time. You had better start getting ready now."

"Bother Mr Potts," grumbled Laura as they went upstairs. She was very tired after her exciting morning and would have liked to take a book and go and read in the hammock.

At three o'clock they were downstairs, looking very clean, neat and well dressed.

Nick had a large sticking-plaster on his knee.

"Are we all ready?" said Gran, coming into the hall. "Yes, you look nice, all of you. Now, please behave yourselves, and don't climb trees or do anything silly this afternoon!"

The children were glad to see that Gran was smiling again. She was never cross for very long as she was very sweet-tempered. They all got into the car and set off.

Mr Potts's house was more like a mansion. It was simply enormous, and the grounds were beautifully laid out. They soon saw the lake that Gran had told them about, and a few small boats moored at the bank.

Mr and Mrs Potts greeted them all very heartily. Mrs Potts was rather large and had more rings on her fingers than Katie had ever seen anyone wear before. She had six ropes of pearls round her neck, and bright earrings dangled in her ears.

"They must be very rich," said Katie to Laura in a low voice. "I wonder what they want to buy Greylings for, when they've got an enormous place like this?"

The children were told that they could go out in the boat, with Mr Potts to help them to row. They would much rather have gone by themselves but it wouldn't have been polite to say so.

They all got into the little boat. It was painted red, and was very pretty. There were two pairs of oars. Nick took one pair and Mr Potts took the other.

"It's quite a way to row round the lake," said Mr Potts. "I'll show you some ducks' nests, and a little waterfall we've made."

It certainly was quite a row round the lake! Katie took the oars after a bit, and then Laura had a turn. They saw three ducks' nests, all with eggs in, and came to the little waterfall, which was very pretty.

Mr Potts talked a lot. He tried to be very nice to them. He noticed Nick's plaster, and spoke to him about it.

"Hurt yourself, Nick?" he asked.

"Nothing much," said Nick.

"He did it this morning," said Laura, who always liked to talk when she could. "He was climbing an enormous tree right to the very top and when he came down, he slipped and grazed his knee badly."

"An enormous tree?" said Mr Potts. "And where was that? In the woods?"

"Yes," said Laura. "Very far into the woods. We followed—"

She stopped and gave a cry of pain. Katie had punched her in the back to stop her saying any more. She knew what Laura was like once she began talking. She never knew when to stop!

"Dear me, why did you stop Laura telling me about your adventures this morning?" asked Mr Potts. "I am most interested. Do go on, my dear."

But Laura would say no more. She bit her lip and hoped that Nick wouldn't scold her afterwards. Why did she always talk too much?

"Well, we'd better be getting back," said Mr Potts, seeing that none of the children were going to say any more about their morning adventures. "I'm afraid this is rather a dull afternoon for you after all your tree-climbing this morning!"

But it wasn't so dull after all, because something most unexpected suddenly happened!

CHAPTER 13

Mr Potts is Clever

Mr Potts and Nick rowed back to the bank. Laura got out first, followed by Katie. Then Nick stood up, but suddenly the boat wobbled violently and Nick fell straight over the side into the water!

It wasn't at all deep and Nick could stand quite easily. But he got a shock and came up gasping and spluttering. Mr Potts looked most alarmed and then helped him to the bank.

"Oh, Nick, are you all right?" cried Laura, who had been really frightened.

"Of course I'm all right!" said Nick, half cross at the fuss. "I can't imagine how I fell in. The boat rocked like anything and I lost my balance, that's all."

Gran and Mrs Potts came hurrying up when they saw what had happened. Mrs Potts was dreadfully upset.

"Oh, my dear boy, you are so wet!" she

cried. "Come along in at once and take your wet things off. We've got some shorts you can borrow, and a tee-shirt and a jumper. Dear, dear, I am sorry this has happened."

"Now don't get upset, my dear," said Mr Potts to his wife. "I'll see to the boy. He won't be any the worse for his wetting, and I can easily get him dry clothing. Come along, Nick. We'll see what we can do for you."

Katie and Laura went with Nick. Mrs Potts sank down on a garden seat, looking quite pale. Gran found that she had to comfort her, because she really looked as if she would burst into tears!

"Such a thing to happen!" she kept saying. "Such a thing to happen!"

Mr Potts took the children into an enormous kitchen and introduced them to a woman sitting at the table. "This is Julie, our housekeeper," he said.

"I'll take his wet clothes off, Mr Potts," said the housekeeper, bustling forward when she saw what had happened.

"No, thank you," said Nick firmly. "I can take them off myself. I hope I won't make your kitchen floor too wet, though."

He stripped off his wet clothes and took the big warm towel that Mr Potts offered him. It wasn't long before he was quite dry. Mr Potts picked up the wet clothes and went through the door with them. "I'll get you some dry ones," he said.

"Oh, sir, don't hang the clothes outside," said Julie, following him. "I'll put them in the drier." But Mr Potts took no notice of her and quickly disappeared. The children found themselves alone.

"Nick! You were silly!" whispered Katie. "It's the first time you've ever fallen out of a boat!"

"And so would you fall out if the boat was rocked violently just as you were standing on one foot, ready to step out," answered Nick crossly. "Mr Potts rocked that boat on purpose. He wanted me to fall into the water!"

"Oh, Nick! But why?" asked Laura, horrified.

"So that I would have to change my wet clothes under his eyes and he could take them away and run through my pockets to see if he could find any signs of the map!" said Nick.

The other two stared at him in silence. They hadn't for one moment thought of such a thing, but they realised that it was likely to be true. After all, the clothes had been whisked off by Mr Potts, despite Julie's offer to help.

"But, Nick," said Katie, beginning to giggle, "you had the false map in your pocket, the one we'd made up!"

"I know that," said Nick with a laugh.

He pulled the big towel round him more closely. "Old Pots-of-Money will have to use his brains to work out that map, won't he?"

"What a good thing you didn't have the proper tracing in your pocket," began Laura. But Nick nudged her, for he had heard footsteps. Julie came in with some dry clothes: some rather big shorts belonging to Mr Potts, a tee-shirt and a yellow sweatshirt.

"Has Mr Potts got my wet clothes?" asked Nick.

"Yes, he has," said Julie indignantly. "He won't let me hang them out, he insists on doing them himself."

Nick winked at the others. "I've no doubt he has some good reason for seeing to them himself," he said. The others giggled.

Nick felt rather odd in his big clothes. Gran laughed when she saw him. Mrs Potts patted him kindly and said, "Well, I expect you'd all like some tea now. Julie's just bringing it out on to the terrace. Come along."

They went to the magnificent terrace that overlooked the lake, and there, set out on low tables, was the most scrumptious tea that the children had ever seen.

There were great ripe strawberries and rich cream. There were the most exciting sandwiches imaginable, honey in the comb looking like golden syrup, a chocolate cake as big as a Christmas cake, little iced cakes of all kinds, a jam sponge stuffed with cream as well, and a plate of the most exciting biscuits. And, to end up with, Julie brought out a dish full of strawberry and vanilla ice creams.

"Wow, this was worth falling into the pond for," said Nick, as he ate his second ice cream, and wished that he could manage a third.

"I'm so glad you enjoyed your tea," said Mrs Potts, who had eaten just as much as the children. Laura thought it wasn't surprising that she was so large, if she ate gorgeous teas like this every day.

The car came round for them after tea and they said goodbye and thank you, and climbed in. Mr Potts promised to send Nick's clothes back the next day.

"That will just give him enough time to dry out our false map and trace it!" said Nick with a grin, as they sat in the car waiting for Gran to finish saying goodbye.

They drove home, feeling rather full. Gran gave a sigh as they turned in at their stone gateposts.

"Dear old Greylings Manor!" she said, as the beautiful old house came into sight. "I am sorry to think you will soon no longer be ours. Mr Potts will be your owner instead!"

"What does old Pots-of-Money want to buy your house for, Gran?" asked Nick. "His own is far bigger and grander."

"Nick! Don't call him that!" said Gran, looking half shocked and half amused. "You must call people by their right names."

"Well, it is his right name," said Nick. "He has got pots of money, hasn't he?"

"Yes, I suppose so," said Gran. "He doesn't want Greylings Manor for himself though, he wants it for his daughter who is getting married soon."

They drove up to the steps and jumped out. "Now you'd better go and do something quiet," said Gran. "After that enormous tea you won't want to climb trees or run races, I hope. And if you don't come to supper, I shall quite understand. I am sure you can't possibly manage any more to eat today!"

But by the time that supper was on the table, the children were quite ready for it. Gran seemed very surprised indeed, but she gave them just as big helpings as usual.

The next day a parcel arrived from Mr Potts. It was Nick's clothes, all dry now, and neatly ironed. He ran his hands through his pockets. Everything was there: string, handkerchief, two bits of toffee, an unusual stone he had picked up, a pencil stump, a broken rubber, a notebook and the map! Yes, that was there as well.

"Carefully copied, I'm quite sure!" said Nick, putting it back again with a grin. "Mr Potts may be smart, but we're smarter! I didn't guess he'd get me into the lake, but we were ready for him anyway. We did that map just in time!"

"I wish tomorrow would come quickly," said Katie. "I want to hunt round that ruined building again – what's left of it! I simply can't think why those steps are shown on the map, if there are none to be seen by the building."

"Perhaps they're not steps," said Nick.

"Well, what else can they be?" asked Laura.

"I can't think!" said Nick, frowning. "No, they must be steps, but there never could have been steps there if the building was on level ground, as it seems to have been."

Katie was thinking hard. She looked up. "I suppose there couldn't have been any steps leading underground from the building, could there?" she asked. "You know, steps going down to a cellar, or something, from inside the building?"

Laura and Nick stared at Katie in surprise. Then Nick smacked his hand down on a nearby table. "Of course!" he said. "Of course! That's what we've got to look for! Steps going down from the building, not steps going up to it! Good thinking, Katie!"

"Tomorrow we'll take forks and spades," said Katie excitedly. "We'll probe all over the ground and see if there are any signs of steps going underground!"

"Now I shan't be able to go to sleep tonight!" said Laura, her eyes shining. "I'll keep on and on thinking of tomorrow!"

CHAPTER 14

AN EXCITING MORNING

The next morning Nick went to ask Mr Tetley to lend him a garden fork and two spades.

"I got into trouble over lending you the axe," said Mr Tetley. "I don't think I'd better lend you anything else."

"Oh, go on, Mr Tetley, please do," begged Katie. She saw Gran in the distance and called to her. "Gran! May we borrow some gardening tools, please? Mr Tetley says he had better not lend them to us."

"Well, so long as it's not an axe or a scythe," said Gran. "I'm glad to hear you want to do some gardening!"

"Dear old Gran's got remarkable hearing," said Nick. "Nobody said a word about doing any gardening! Anyway, Mr Tetley, please can we have those things, now that Gran's given the okay?"

Mr Tetley handed them over, and they

marched off with the tools, hoping that Gran wouldn't call them and ask where they were going to garden. Nick slipped indoors for his torch. He thought that if they did find steps going underground they would need some light!

"We'll go the short way," said Nick. "We won't scramble all through the woods again. Where's Russet? Hi, Russet, come on, you can take us the way you took us yesterday!"

As they marched down the drive to the gates, Mr Potts's car came in. Mr Potts saw the children and stopped the car.

"I just came to ask if Nick was all right after his wetting yesterday," he said, showing all his white teeth in a wide smile. "But you are, Nick. Dear me, wherever are you going with those spades and forks?"

The children couldn't think what to say. Then Nick spoke up. "We're going to the farm," he said. This was quite true. They had to pass the farm, and they meant to call in for a moment to see Mrs Taylor.

"Oh! You're going to help the farmer, are you?" said Mr Potts. This wasn't exactly a question, so nobody answered it. But Laura, of course, went as red as a tomato. She always did if she felt awkward or guilty about anything. Mr Potts noticed her red face at once.

"Have you found the other piece of that map?" he said suddenly.

Now this was a very difficult question to answer. If Nick said yes, Mr Potts would ask him for it and would see that it was different from the copy he had found in Nick's pocket. If he said no, it was a lie, and Nick, like the others, hated lies.

The three stared at Mr Potts, quite tongue-tied – and then Russet saved them! He suddenly saw a stray hen and barked loudly at it. He rushed at it, and the frightened creature fluttered into the hedge.

"Excuse us, Mr Potts. We must rescue the hen!" cried Nick thankfully, and he darted off. The others went too and left Mr Potts in the car, looking annoyed.

"Quick, Russet, scare the hen through the hedge," whispered Laura, "then we can squeeze through after it and disappear!"

Russet was delighted to find that for a change the children were encouraging him to bark at a hen, instead of scolding him for it. He went completely mad, barked his head almost off and made the hen almost faint with fear. The children made as much noise as they could too, shouting to the hen and one another, as they pretended to shoo away Russet and catch the poor hen.

They squeezed through the hedge, and although they could hear Mr Potts calling to them, they took no notice and shouted all the more loudly. At last they began to giggle. Nick hurriedly picked up the hen, and tore off with it, afraid that Mr Potts would leave the car and come after them.

But he didn't. They heard the car going up the drive. Nick set the hen down when he came to the hen-run, and it ran to join the others, squawking loudly.

"Poor old hen!" said Laura, sorry for the clucking bird. "But it did save us from a very awkward moment."

"It did," said Nick. "Come on. We'd better slip off quickly before old Pots-of-Money catches us again."

So once more they set off, this time without any interruption. They came to the Taylors' house, and stopped for a few minutes to talk to Mrs Taylor. She was surprised to see their spades and fork.

"What in the world are you going to do?" she asked.

"It's a secret, Mrs Taylor!" said Laura. "We'll tell you all about it one day."

"All right, I'll wait till then!" said the farmer's wife. "Would you like some of my freshly baked cakes?"

"Well, if you'd like us to take a few with us, we'd be very pleased," said Nick. "But we can't stop long today, because we have a busy morning in front of us!"

"I'll pop some into a bag for you," said Mrs Taylor kindly, and she put in at least a dozen.

They set off again with Russet, who was very interested in the bag of cakes. Nick sent him on in front, hoping that he would be sensible enough to take them the way they had come yesterday.

He did take them the right way. He was a very clever dog, and loved trying to read the children's thoughts. He trotted ahead, and it wasn't long before the children came to the humpy hill, and found the place where they had uncovered so many old grey stones the day before.

"Now the thing to do is to jab about with

138

the fork and see what we can feel underneath all this moss and stuff growing on what must have been the floor of the building," said Nick. So, taking the long-pronged fork, he began to jab strongly here and there. Each time he jabbed, the fork struck something hard. He stopped, and looked at the others. "There must be a proper floor underneath here," he said. "A tiled floor perhaps, like our secret house has. We'll clear it if we can."

Nick was right. Under the moss, the grass and the bracken was a tiled floor. The tiles were small, and even after so many years were still bright in colour. Russet helped as much as he could, scraping away excitedly.

After a great deal of hard work, the children had most of the floor uncovered. Many of the tiles were broken. Some were missing altogether. Then Katie uncovered a flat slab of stone, quite different from the coloured tiles. "Look!" she cried. "Here's something different. A big slab of stone that's got some sort of pattern on it."

Laura and Nick came beside Katie to see what the pattern was. Laura gave a shout.

"Don't you know what the pattern is? It's the Greylings eagle, just like the ones on the gateposts, only flat instead of rounded. That shows this was a Greylings building."

"Why do you suppose they placed a flat stone here suddenly, in the middle of the coloured tiles?" asked Katie. "It seems odd to me."

"It is odd," said Nick. "But I bet I can explain the oddness! The flight of steps must be underneath that slab!"

"Wow!" said Laura and Katie in delight. "Fantastic!"

"The thing is, how are we going to lift it?" said Nick. "It looks very heavy. I wonder if there's an iron ring or anything that we can pull it up by? Let's clear the whole slab properly and see."

They cleared it from end to end, but there was no iron ring anywhere. Nick stood on the slab and jumped on it to see if he could make it move.

The slab moved at once. There was a creaking, cracking noise as if something underneath was breaking, and Nick leaped off the slab in alarm. The children stared at it. Something below the slab of stone had given way, and now it was lying crookedly below the surface of the floor.

"Now what did it do that for?" said Nick. "It did give me a shock when it moved like that, and did you hear that funny breaking noise?"

"Perhaps the stone was placed on wooden supports," said Laura. "And maybe they have rotted with the years, and when you jumped on the stone, the wood cracked and gave way."

"I think you're right," said Nick, kicking at the stone with his foot. "I don't like to tread on it again. I wonder how we could move it?"

"There's a big stone over there, that was once part of the wall," said Katie. "I think we could all three carry it between us and drop it down on the slab to see if that would move it!"

"Good idea," said Nick. They went to the big square stone and with great difficulty lifted it up. They staggered with it to the slab and then, at a word from Nick, dropped it right onto the flat stone.

The result was startling. The heavy stone

struck the slab, which gave way and, with a crash, disappeared entirely, taking the heavy stone with it! The children found themselves staring into a black hole!

"Wow!" said Nick in the greatest astonishment. "Look at that!"

"The flight of steps must be down there," said Katie excitedly. She bent over to see. Nick took out his little torch and flashed it into the hole.

They saw an old stairway leading

downwards into the darkness.

"So we were right!" said Laura, in delight. "Down there must be where the Greylings Treasure is hidden!"

Laura was so excited that she almost fell down the hole. Nick pulled her back. "Don't be an idiot!" he said. "The whole place is rotten with age and if you miss your step you'll crash to the bottom and hurt yourself."

They examined the entrance where the slab had been, and saw that the flat stone had rested on wood which, as Laura had said, had become rotten, and had given way under Nick's weight.

"I want to go down the steps," said Laura. "Nick, do let me be the first one."

"No, don't!" said Nick. "Those steps look all right, but they may be quite rotten too. I shall try them first."

"Well, be careful then, Nick," said Katie anxiously.

Nick stuck his torch in his pocket and sat down at the entrance to the hole. He tried the top step with his foot. With a crack it broke away at once, and the splinters went down below. Nick tried the next step. That broke too. The steps were as rotten as deadwood in a tree struck by lightning.

"Blow! The steps are no use at all," said Nick. "They wouldn't bear the weight of a mouse!"

"How can we get down then?" asked Laura, so anxious to explore underground that she couldn't keep still.

"We'll have to get a rope," said Nick. Laura and Katie looked very disappointed. They couldn't bear the thought of going home and leaving the exciting hole even for an hour!

"Couldn't we jump down and chance it?" said Katie.

"Don't be a fool!" said Nick. "You'd probably break your leg and then we'd have to go for help. Russet, get away or you'll fall in."

"Well, let's go home quickly and get the rope," said Katie impatiently. "Anyway, it's almost lunch-time. We'd better not be late again. We can come back afterwards."

"Come on, then," said Nick, and glanced at his watch. "Oh, no! We're late again! Run!"

CHAPTER 15

An Unexpected Punishment

They hadn't gone very far before a thought came into Katie's head. "Oh, listen," she said, stopping. "Do you think we ought to leave that hole open like that? Suppose someone came along and saw it, and got down before we did?"

"Yes, you're right," said Nick. "We ought to throw bracken and branches over it to hide it. Let's go back and do it quickly. It won't take a minute!"

But a nasty surprise awaited them as they made their way back through the trees. The sound of voices came to them!

Nick put his hand on Russet's collar at once, in case he should bark.

"Shh!" he said to the others. "Don't make a sound. Take Russet, Laura, and I'll creep up and see who it is."

Nick crept silently from bush to bush, keeping himself completely hidden, and at last he came in sight of the ruined building. He had a dreadful shock! Mr Potts was there, with another man! They were looking at the hole and talking in excitement.

"Those children are smart!" said Mr Potts. "They've found the very place. That map in the boy's pocket was wrong. We've been on a regular wild-goose chase this morning, following goodness knows how many bends in the stream! It's a good thing we heard their voices, and came to see what they were doing!"

"We'd never have found this by ourselves," said the second man. "This little hill is well hidden, and the old building has fallen to pieces. Those are the steps shown in the map, Potts, no doubt of it. But they're quite rotten. We'd better come back again with a rope."

"Well, those kids will be back after lunch," said Mr Potts, rubbing his chin and thinking. "Let me see, how can we stop them? I know! I'll get my wife to phone up the old lady and invite the children to go for a picnic somewhere! Then they'll be out of the way. I can't come back here after lunch, as I've business to see to, but we'll be here early in the morning before those kids are about."

"Come on then," said the other man. "I wish I knew a short way back. I'm soaked to the knees from that marshy bit!"

Nick couldn't help grinning. He wasn't going to show them the other way back! He waited until the men had disappeared round the humpy hill and then he shot back to the others. He told them all he had heard. They listened in rage.

"Well!" said Katie. "So he thinks he'll get the treasure before we do, does he? He thinks he'll get us nicely out of the way for the rest of the day! Well, he won't. We'll refuse to go on the picnic!"

"Absolutely," said Laura. "We have to get here this afternoon. Then, when he arrives early tomorrow morning, he'll find nothing at all!"

"Hey, we must go!" said Nick. "It's five to one! You know what a row we got into yesterday!" They raced home, carrying the spades and fork, hoping Gran wouldn't be too cross.

But she was. She was very angry indeed

and, worse still, Grandad was in a rage as well.

"Half past one!" said Grandad, as they trooped into the hall. "Is that what you call being punctual? Two days running! It's disgraceful! Really disgraceful!"

"We're awfully sorry, Grandad," said Nick.

"Being sorry isn't enough," said Grandad, looking really fierce. "Your grandmother gets nice meals for you and then you keep us waiting like this."

"It is very naughty of you all," said Gran. "I've a good mind to take the lunch away and make you have bread and cheese, but I'm sure you are all very hungry, and I don't like to do that."

"But you'll be punished all the same!" said Grandad, looking very fierce still. "Oh, yes! You'll go up to your rooms after lunch and there you'll stay for the rest of the day. You'll have your tea up there and no supper! Bad children! I'm very angry with you!"

Grandad stalked out of the hall and the children stared after him in dismay. What! Spend the rest of the day in their bedrooms, when they had such important work to do after lunch? They couldn't!

"Grandad!" called Nick. "Please forgive us. Just this once. You see—"

"I never listen to excuses," said Grandad. "You'll do as you are told and say no more."

Laura began to cry with tiredness and disappointment. She stamped her foot. "It's too bad, it's too bad!" she shouted. "Grandad, you're unkind! You ought to listen to Nick."

"Laura!" said Grandad, in a shocked voice. "Don't be rude. I'll send you all up to your rooms immediately if I have any more nonsense."

Laura didn't want to make the other two lose their lunch, so she wiped her eyes and said no more. They went meekly into the dining-room and sat down.

"You mustn't make Grandad angry by arguing with him, Laura," said Gran, serving out big helpings of cold meat, potatoes and salad. "You have been very thoughtless, coming in late like this again, and you deserve to be punished. Now, I don't want to hear a word from you. Eat up your lunch quietly."

Gran took up the paper and sat down. The children were very hungry indeed, and they ate quickly. Just as Gran had finished ladling out the raspberries and cream for pudding, the telephone rang.

Jane came into the room after a minute. "Mr Potts is on the phone for you, Mrs Greyling," she said. Gran got up and went into the hall, where the phone was. She left the door open, and the children could hear every word she said.

"Good afternoon, Mr Potts," she said. Then she listened. "Oh, it's very kind of Mrs Potts to offer to take the children for such a lovely picnic, but I'm sorry to say they can't come. No, they really can't, Mr Potts . . . No, they're not ill – as a matter of fact, they have been rather naughty, and they have been told to keep to their rooms for the rest of the day. What? Yes, I'm afraid they will be indoors . . . No, they will not be allowed out at all – so you see they can't possibly go to the picnic, but please thank Mrs Potts for me. Another day, perhaps."

Then Gran listened again as Mr Potts spoke for some time.

"Well, I'm glad you have definitely

decided to buy Greylings," said Gran. "Yes, the papers will be ready for us to sign tomorrow. Our solicitor will be here, and if you like to come tomorrow morning at ten o'clock, the whole matter can be finally settled . . . Yes, yes. Goodbye."

Gran put back the receiver. The children longed to speak to one another and say what they thought, but they had been told not to talk. And everything was to be settled at ten o'clock tomorrow morning. It was dreadful. Tears trickled down poor Laura's face and fell into her raspberries.

Gran came back. "Mrs Potts wanted to know if you could go for a picnic with her this afternoon," she said. "Now you see what you have missed by being so silly!"

"I don't want to go picnicking with Mrs Potts," said Laura. "I'm glad we're not going! I don't like Mr and Mrs Pots-of-Money!"

"Laura! Don't talk like that!" said Gran sharply.

"Gran, please don't let them buy it!" said Nick. "We're going to find the treasure for you, really we are!"

"Don't talk nonsense, dear," said Gran.

"I suppose you are thinking of that old map? Well, I'm sure it doesn't mean anything at all."

"Oh, but, Gran, really we—" began Nick, but Gran wouldn't let him say any more.

"That's quite enough, Nick," she said. "Have you all finished? Go up to your rooms then. And remember you are to stay there for the rest of the day. Tea will be sent up to you, but you'll have to go without supper, and I hope you will remember that when you are guests in somebody's house the least you can do is be punctual for meals!"

"We're very sorry, Gran," said Katie humbly, hoping that Gran would change her mind. "Couldn't we just stay in our rooms till teatime and then take Russet for a walk?"

"Certainly not," said Grandad, who had come in at that moment. "I never heard of such a thing! Go along now, and can I trust you not to leave your rooms, or must you be locked in?"

"You can trust us," said Laura, her cheeks going red. "We promise to stay in our rooms for the rest of the day."

"Very well," said Grandad. "I trust you. The Greylings never break their word."

The children went upstairs slowly and sadly. They sat in the girls' room and looked at one another miserably.

"This is the worst bit of luck that could happen!" said Nick. "Who would have thought Grandad would be so fierce?"

"Well, what about Gran?" said Katie. "She was fierce too. And all the time we're trying so hard to find the treasure for them."

"Yes, but grown-ups don't think of things like that," said Nick. "Oh, don't cry, Laura. I can't bear to lose the treasure either, but it's worse for you because you are a Greyling."

There was a scraping at the door, and Russet whined outside.

"Good old Russet!" said Katie, jumping up. "He wants to share our punishment too!"

Russet came in and jumped up on to Nick's knee. He licked the boy's chin.

"Nick, Laura, I suppose we can't possibly go to the woods?" said Katie, in a timid voice. "I feel as if we must. Don't you think

Grandad would understand, once we had got the treasure?"

"I know Grandad well enough to know that he would rather lose the treasure than have any of us breaking our word," said Laura. "We've promised, Katie, and we can't possibly break a promise."

"Laura's absolutely right, Katie," said Nick. "Don't even think of it! It would be an awful thing to do, and we'd hate ourselves for it."

"Yes, I suppose so," said Katie in a miserable voice. "Oh, how I wish Mr Potts was at the bottom of his own stupid lake!"

That made Nick laugh. "That's where he tried to put me yesterday!" he said. "Well, old Pots-of-Money knows we are well out of the way now, picnic or no picnic, so he's safe to attend to his business this afternoon."

"I'm tired," said Laura. "I'm going to lie on my bed and have a nap."

But no sooner had she lain down than an idea came to her. She jumped off her bed and called to the others.

"I've got an idea!" she said.

CHAPTER 16

AN UNDERGROUND ADVENTURE

Nick and Katie looked at Laura. "What is it?" asked Nick doubtfully. He didn't think there could be any good ideas just at that moment.

"Well, listen, Nick," said Laura. "We've promised to stay in our rooms for the rest of the day, haven't we?"

"Yes," said Nick and Katie nodded.

"But we haven't promised to stay in them all *night* long!" cried Laura. "Mr Potts is going to explore that underground place early in the morning. Why can't we go there tonight? We can take torches. We'll be quite all right. It would be just as dark down in that hole in the daytime as in the night, so it won't make a bit of difference, really."

"Well! That is an idea!" said Nick, really excited. "Why didn't we think of it before? We shan't be breaking any promises if we go there after midnight!"

"We'll go!" shouted Katie. "What an adventure it'll be!"

"We'll creep down the secret stairs so that no one will hear us," said Nick. "We'll take our torches, and we'll find a strong rope."

"We'll get the treasure before old Pots-of-Money!" shouted Katie.

"Great!" said Laura, delighted that her idea was approved of. "But you'll tell everyone in the house what we're going to do if you shout like that!"

"I feel much happier now," said Katie. "What shall we do till teatime?"

"I think we'd better try and have a nap," said Nick, "if we're going to be up half the night!" So they all three lay on their beds and shut their eyes.

The smell of the early roses outside the window came into their rooms. Bees hummed loudly. Everything was peaceful, and soon the children, happy again now, were fast asleep. They had worked so hard that morning, digging and scraping, that they were really tired out. They did not wake until Jane came knocking at the girls' door with their tea. She came in and put the tray down on the table.

"And what have you been doing to get sent to your rooms like this?" she said. "Late for lunch again, I suppose. There's nothing that makes your grandfather crosser than that!"

"Oooh, what a nice tea you have brought us, Jane!" said Laura, looking at the tray of things. "Egg sandwiches – my favourite! And what are these? – Cheese and pickle. Thank you!"

"And ginger biscuits and chocolate cake!" said Katie. "Well, I shan't mind going without any supper now."

"You'll never be able to eat all this," said Jane. "I'll fetch your tray later."

"Thanks, Jane," said Nick.

Jane left the room, and the three children began their tea. They enjoyed it. They talked about what they were going to do that night. It was very exciting.

"I think we'd better keep some cake for tonight," said Katie. "We'll be terribly hungry if we go exploring at midnight!"

So they cut three enormous slices and put them in the top drawer of the chest.

"Good heavens!" Jane said, when she

came in and saw what a lot they had eaten. "Nearly everything gone! You won't miss your suppers!"

She went, carrying the tray. The children found some cards and played card games until seven o'clock. Then Gran came in.

"Well," she said, "I'm sorry to have had to punish you like this, but you will please remember in future not to be late for your meals, won't you?"

"Yes, Gran," they all said.

"You'd better go to bed now," said Gran. "You're not coming down for supper, so I'll say goodnight, and I hope tomorrow you'll turn over a new leaf, and we'll all be happy together again. It upsets me to have to treat you like this, but I promised your mother I wouldn't spoil you."

They said goodnight to Gran and listened to her going down the stairs to the hall. "It's not worth while getting undressed," said Laura.

"Well, we'd better," said Nick. "Gran may come up again for something, or even Grandad, and we don't want to get into any trouble. We can easily dress again before midnight."

So they undressed and got into bed. But none of them could go to sleep! They talked to one another and listened to the hall clock chiming the hours and the half-hours.

"Gran's gone to bed now," said Laura. "I heard her door click. It must be eleven o'clock."

The children talked quietly until they heard the hall clock chime twelve, then they slipped out of bed.

"Don't make a sound," said Nick. "If we drop anything on the floor it may wake Gran or Grandad up."

So they were very quiet indeed, and were soon dressed. Nick took the slices of cake out of the drawer and they ate all of them. The cake tasted delicious at that time of the night! "We had some supper after all," said Katie, with a grin.

They opened Nick's cupboard, and one by one they tiptoed down the tiny winding stairway to the dining-room. From there they crept round to the garden door at the side of the house. They unlocked it and stepped outside.

"The moon's full tonight," said Nick. "We're in luck!" The moonlight lay on the ground like pools of silvery water.

"Where's Russet?" asked Nick. "He's kept amazingly quiet."

"Just behind me," answered Laura. "He can't imagine what we're doing but he's delighted to go for a moonlight walk!"

"Now for a rope," said Nick. They went to the garden shed and shone their torches round. They found quite a big coil in one corner. It was thick and strong, just what they wanted.

Nick picked it up. It was heavy. He flung it over his shoulder, and thought he could carry it quite easily like that. Then, with Russet at their heels, they set off for the Taylors' farm, and the ruined building.

They only needed their torches in the shadowy woods, where the dense trees hid the moon. When finally they arrived at the hole, they had to clear away the branches and bracken that Mr Potts had put there to stop anyone else finding it.

"At least we know no one is in there," said Katie, heaving the last branch away.

"I'll go down first," said Nick. He tied the rope to a tree-trunk nearby, and let the other end fall into the hole. Then he let himself carefully down the rope, swung on it, and slid slowly to the ground below.

"Come on! The bottom's not too far below," he shouted to the others, flashing his torch around. "There's a passage here. It smells a bit musty, but it's fine, not blocked up, or anything."

The others slid down the rope. Nick helped Laura, who was too excited to take proper care. They all three switched on their torches and looked around.

In front of them was a narrow passage, with the roof just above their heads.

"I believe it leads into that hill!" said Nick. "You know, the little humpy hill."

He was right, it did! The children followed the passage, which was very narrow in parts, and at last came out into a curious oblong room, hewn out of the very heart of the hill. It was strange to stand there in the light of their torches, and look round at a room where no one had been for so many years.

"This must have been a hiding place for the Greylings at some time or other," said Nick. "In the old days people were often ill-treated because of their religion, and maybe this room was a hidy-hole for a long-ago Greyling. It's a marvellous place, right in the heart of the wood, and in the heart of the hill!"

"Where's the treasure, do you suppose?" asked Katie, looking round. They flashed their torches everywhere. The room was furnished very plainly with strong wooden benches and a narrow table. On a shelf plates and mugs still stood, dusty and cobwebby. The floor was tiled like the floor above. There was no fireplace at all.

"I can't see anywhere for treasure to be hidden," said Nick. "Wouldn't it be disappointing to have followed all this way to the very end of the map, and find that the treasure wasn't here after all!"

"Look, there's an old wooden door in that corner," said Laura, suddenly. She shone her torch there and Katie and Nick saw what she meant. They hadn't noticed the door before, because the earthen walls matched the brown of the wooden door.

"Perhaps it's a cupboard!" said Nick in excitement. He went over to the door. It was shut fast, and seemed to be bolted on the other side.

"Strange," said Nick. "How could it be bolted the other side? People wouldn't bolt themselves in a cupboard, surely?"

"The door is as rotten as those steps were," said Katie. She aimed a kick at the lower part. It gave way and the wood broke at once. Katie kicked again, and soon there was an enormous hole in the door!

Nick put his hand in at the hole and felt about for bolts. He found them but they were too stiff to undo. So he and Katie kicked at the door until it was almost kicked away, and the three children could easily squeeze through the hole.

It wasn't a cupboard. It was the entrance to another passage, a little wider than the first one, and leading in the opposite direction.

"Come on. Let's see if we can find anything here," said Nick. He walked a few steps and then came to a stop. In his way, blocking the passage, lay a great wooden box, with bands of iron round it. The lock had rusted and the lid was loose.

The children shone their torches on it and looked at one another, excitedly. Was it – could it be – the treasure, at last?

CHAPTER 17

The Treasure at Last!

Laura bent over the chest. "I hardly dare lift up the lid in case the box is empty!" she said in a whisper. Nobody knew why she whispered, but it seemed the right thing to do. She lifted up the lid, and then – oh, what a marvellous sight!

The Greylings Treasure lay inside the old chest. Somehow or other the dust and the damp had kept away from the box, and the treasure shone undimmed. Sparkling brooches, wonderful necklaces, jewelled pins – and loveliest of all, the magnificent Greylings Cup made of pure gold, with its centre and base studded with precious stones! Laura lifted it out.

"Look!" she said. "Oh, look! The very cup that we saw in that old book. The lucky cup! It's been here for years and years. Oh, what will Gran say? She'll be rich! She won't need to sell Greylings after all!"

She handed the cup to Nick and knelt down by the box with Katie. They put their fingers among the jewels.

"Pearls for Gran! Brooches for Mum! Lots of lovely things for everyone," Laura said. "Oooh! This is wonderful! How clever we are to have found it."

"Yes, I think we are," said Nick. "After all, people have been hunting for this lost treasure for three hundred years, and now three children have found it!"

"Won't Mr Potts be angry when he hears that we got here first?" said Katie. "And he'll be angrier still when he finds that Gran won't need to sell her lovely old house to him after all! Oh, I'm longing to get home and wake up Gran and Grandad and tell them everything!"

"Listen," said Nick suddenly. "What's that noise?"

They all listened. "It's Russet barking," said Laura in surprise. "What's he barking at?"

"Suppose somebody is coming through the woods," said Katie, clutching Nick. "Suppose it's Mr Potts and the other man, coming earlier than they said? What will they do when they find us here?"

Nick ran back into the oblong room, and then made his way down the first passage. He shone his torch up to the top of the entrance hole. Russet looked down, wagging his tail. He gave a short yelp. "Is there somebody coming, Russet?" said Nick. "Come on down with me. Jump!"

Russet jumped into Nick's arms. Nick listened and at last caught the noise of people scrambling through the woods! In the silent night the sound could be heard very clearly.

Nick thought quickly. There was no time to escape. Was there any good hiding place for them up the second passage? Could they take the treasure with them and hide it? How could they carry that heavy box?

He took out his penknife and cut a long piece from the rope that hung through the hole. It might be useful. Then, hearing voices coming nearer, he shot back to the others.

"Sounds like Potts and one or two more," he said. "Come on. Let's see if this passage has got any sort of hiding place for us."

"How are we going to take the treasure with us?" asked Laura.

Nick quickly tied the rope round the big box. He knotted it at the top leaving two long ends, which he looped firmly. He gave one loop to Katie and took the other himself. "We can carry the box between us," he said. "It's too heavy for one person, but we can easily carry it like this, swung on the rope."

"Good idea," said Katie. "Get out of the way, Russet. You don't want this box on your head!"

Laura had crept to the oblong room and was listening to see what was happening. She heard somebody at the entrance to the hole.

"Hello! Look here!" came Mr Potts's voice. "Somebody's dropped a rope down. I didn't see it this morning, did you?"

"No," said another voice. "I suppose those kids aren't down there, are they?"

"They'll be sorry if they are!" said Mr Potts in an angry voice. "Making false maps and trying to throw us off the trail, stupid little fools!"

Laura didn't wait to hear any more. She

fled up the second passage to tell the others.

"Oh, here you are," said Nick impatiently. "We wondered where you were. Don't go disappearing like that when we've got to escape."

Laura told the others what she had heard. The three of them set off up the second passage, Nick and Katie carrying the box between them.

"I only hope this passage leads somewhere!" said Nick. Their three torches threw a bright light up the dark tunnel which was musty and, in places, very low. It ran straight for some time, then turned to the left. Suddenly the passage split into two, one way turning to the right and the other going straight on.

"Oh no!" said Nick. "Which way should we go, I wonder?"

Katie anxiously shone her torch up first one way and then the other. "The right-hand one seems a bit wider," she said. "Let's go that way."

"Okay," said Nick. "Laura, have you got a handkerchief? Good! Throw it down on the ground just a little way up the other passage, will you?"

"Whatever for?" asked Laura in surprise.

"So that old Pots-of-Money will think we've gone up that way, and follow the wrong path," said Nick.

Laura laughed. "You are clever, Nick!" she said.

She threw her white handkerchief down on the ground a little way up the passage. Then the three of them, with Russet nuzzling against their legs, took the right-hand tunnel.

It went on and on. Once they came to where part of the roof had fallen in, and had to climb over a heap of stones and earth.

"I feel like a rabbit running through a burrow," whispered Laura.

"With foxes behind us," said Katie softly.

"Oh don't!" said Laura. "I hope Mr Potts has gone up the wrong passage."

Mr Potts had. He and his friends – there were two of them this time – had jumped down the hole, found the strange underground room, and squeezed through the broken door that led up the second passage. But when they came to the splitting of the ways, they'd caught sight of Laura's handkerchief, just as Nick had hoped they would.

"They've gone up there," said Mr Potts. And up the wrong passage they went! But before they had gone very far the passage came to an end in a small cupboard-like room, the walls of which were stone. It was quite empty, though Mr Potts wasted several minutes trying to see if any of the stones might reveal a hiding place.

By the time that Mr Potts and his friends had turned back and started to follow the other passage, the three treasure-finders had got a long way ahead.

"I can't think where this is leading to," said Nick, putting down the box for a moment. It was very heavy, and though he and Katie were strong, their arms were aching badly.

They went on again after a bit. Russet ran ahead, thinking that all this was a fine adventure! Every time he turned round his eyes gleamed like the headlights of a small car in the light of their torches.

Suddenly the passage came to an end, and facing the children were a few rough steps of stone.

"What a relief!" said Nick. "We've got somewhere at last."

Katie shone her torch overhead. The stone steps led to a square stone slab that lay flat in the earthy roof above their heads.

"Why, it looks as if there's a slab of stone at the entrance here, just like the one we moved at the beginning," said Nick.

"But not nearly so big," said Katie. "Come up the steps, Nick, and try to push up the stone with me."

They both went up the steps. They bent double and heaved with their backs against the slab. It seemed to move a little.

"Nick! Katie! They're coming! I can hear them!" suddenly cried Laura. "We shall be caught. Oh, do hurry!"

There was the sound of voices and footsteps to be heard a good way along the passage. Nick and Katie pushed at the stone slab with all their strength. Russet ran back along the passage, barking loudly and fiercely.

"That's right, Russet! Keep them there! Don't let them pass!" shouted Laura. Russet felt very fierce. He tore down the passage till he saw Mr Potts and his friends and then the brave little dog stood in front of them, barking, growling, and showing his teeth. He would not let them pass!

The children heard Mr Potts's voice shouting to them:

"You wicked children! What are you doing here at this time of night? Call your dog off. He's making himself a nuisance!"

The children didn't say a word. Nick heaved with all his might and the roots of the grasses that had been clinging to the stone slab and keeping it tightly in place all gave way. The stone lifted up and Nick put his head out into the cool night air!

The children all climbed out of the hole, and stood in the bright moonlight for a moment, wondering where they were. And then Nick suddenly knew!

"We're near Mr Taylor's Farm!" he cried. "Look, there it is, beyond the field gate. We've come up into that ruined stone hut we saw the other day in the field. How incredible! There's an underground way between the old building in the woods and this one, and we've found it!"

"Oh, do come on," said Katie, who was very afraid of being caught. "Let's go down to the farm and wake Mrs Taylor up. She'll look after us!"

"Come on then," said Nick, thinking it would be very nice to see plump Mrs Taylor. They half stumbled, half ran down the field, Nick and Katie still carrying the box between them.

When they came to the pigsty, Nick put the box down. "Let's hide the treasure here," he said. "Nobody would guess it was in a pigsty!"

So under the straw of the pigsty went the old box. The pigs grunted sleepily in surprise. Nick stood up and stretched his tired back.

"Look! There are Mr Potts and his friends, just climbing out," he said. "Let's go and wake up the farmer! I think I'd like someone grown-up on our side now!"

CHAPTER 18

SAFE AT THE TAYLORS' FARM

In the bright moonlight the children could see the three men running over the sloping field towards them, but they still had some distance to go, and the children reached the farmhouse well before them.

"Come on, let's bang on the door," said Nick. "No one will find the treasure in the pigsty."

They ran round the farmhouse, and Nick banged on the big knocker there. The sound thundered through the night. *Crash*! *Crash*! *Crash*! A window was flung open and the farmer looked out in astonishment.

"Who's there?" he shouted.

"It's us!" shouted back Nick. "We're in trouble – somebody's chasing us. Please let us in!"

"Good gracious! It's the children from Greylings!" said Mrs Taylor's voice, and her head appeared by the side of the farmer's.

"I'll go down and let them in, Fred."

In half a minute the big bolts were being drawn back, and the great wooden door was opened. The children pressed inside and Nick banged the door. He could see the three men running up the path.

"Now, my dears, what's all this?" said Mrs Taylor, in amazement. She didn't look a bit like herself because she was wearing an enormous white nightgown, with a pink shawl thrown over it, and her hair was done up in four tight plaits that stuck out round her plump red face.

Before the children could answer there came another knocking at the door. Mrs Taylor jumped.

"Bless us all!" she said. "Who's that now?"

The farmer came into the hall; he had pulled on his trousers, and put on some bedroom slippers. He looked just as amazed as his wife.

"Fred! There's someone at the door again!" said Mrs Taylor.

"Aye! I can hear them," said the farmer. "I'll open up before they knock my door down."

The children went into the big kitchen with Mrs Taylor. She poked the fire, which was still showing red.

"Why, you're shivering!" she said, looking at them. "You can't be cold this warm night."

"We're shivering with excitement," said Laura. "Oh, Mrs Taylor, take care of us, won't you?"

"Of course, of course," said Mrs Taylor, in still greater surprise. "You're safe here."

The farmer brought Mr Potts and his two friends into the kitchen. Mr Potts looked very angry. He glared at the three children, who stood close to Mrs Taylor.

"Now what's all this about?" asked Mr Taylor, looking sternly at the three men. "Have you been frightening these children?"

"Let me explain," said Mr Potts. "I have bought Greylings Manor, and—"

"You haven't bought it yet!" said Nick.

"Don't interrupt, my boy!" said Mr Potts. "The final papers are being signed tomorrow, but I regard myself as the owner of the Greylings Estate now. Everything's settled."

"Well, what's all that got to do with you being out at this time of night?" asked Mr Taylor.

"My friends and I are interested in the old ruins belonging to Greylings," said Mr Potts. "Naturally those belong to us, as well as the house and the grounds. Well, we have been doing a little exploring, and these children have very strangely and rudely been trying to interfere with our affairs. My friend here is an authority on old books, china, jewellery, and so on, and I have promised to let him have any old Greylings property to examine."

"You're not telling the story truthfully," said Nick, boiling with rage.

"My dear boy, don't be rude," said Mr Potts. "As you can see, Mr Taylor, these children are quite out of hand. We have been looking for some old things that belong to the property, and we have reason to believe that these children have stolen them tonight. This is a very serious matter, but if the children are willing to hand us back our property now, we will not make any more trouble over it."

"They didn't bring anything in here with

them at all," said Mrs Taylor. "And let me tell you, sir, that these children are not the sort to steal! I never heard of such a thing!"

"Mrs Taylor! It was the Greylings Treasure we found!" said Laura. "It's Gran's and Grandad's! It doesn't belong to Mr Potts. We found it tonight! They were after it too, these three men!"

"The Greylings Treasure!" said Mrs Taylor, in astonishment. "Well, I never did! The Greylings Treasure! Are you sure?"

"Quite sure," said Laura. "We looked it up in an old book, and saw the pictures of some of the things, and they were there, in the old box!"

"Well, my girl, you must let us have the box," said Mr Potts. "I tell you, I have bought Greylings, and anything found on the property is mine. You will get into serious trouble over this if you don't give me what belongs to me."

"That's so," said one of the men.

"I don't care!" Laura almost shouted. "You can't have it!"

"Well, give us the box to put somewhere safe just for tonight," said Mr Potts. "Then tomorrow we'll all look into the matter with your grandmother and grandfather. Now, be sensible children and tell us where you put the treasure."

"Well, I think maybe you'd better do that," said Mr Taylor. "If this gentleman has bought the property, you'd better be careful."

"We will *not* give up the treasure!" said Nick.

"No, we won't!" cried Laura and Katie. They were all quite sure about that.

"Then we shall find it ourselves," said Mr Potts, looking furious. "And you'll get into trouble, all three of you. I'll see that you do, you interfering little wretches!"

The men went into the hall and out of the front door. They began to hunt about in the moonlight for the box of treasure. The children flew to the window of the front room and watched them. Would they look in the big pigsty?

They did go to it, but the sty smelled and the men didn't even open the gate. They did not think for one moment that the children would have chosen such a peculiar place!

Mr Potts suddenly grew tired of the

search. "Come on," he said to the others. "We'll have something to say about this tomorrow!"

To the children's great delight they saw the three men going away. Then, and not till then, did they pour out their extraordinary story to Mrs Taylor and the astonished farmer.

Nick and Katie went out to the pigsty to get the box. It was covered with straw, and did not smell very nice, but nobody minded! How the children enjoyed Mr Taylor's surprise when they opened the box and displayed the marvellous things inside! Mrs Taylor couldn't believe her eyes. She would not even touch the things, she just stared and stared at them, saying, "I never saw such things! Never in my life!" over and over again.

"So, you see, we've got the lost treasure at last!" said Laura, dancing round the kitchen. "Isn't it fantastically exciting, Mrs Taylor?"

"I never heard of such a thing!" said Mrs Taylor, and her plump face looked even redder than usual with the surprise and excitement.

"Well, I'm going to take you children back home," said Mr Taylor, getting up.

"Oh, couldn't they stay here for the night?" said Mrs Taylor. "They'll be tired out."

The children thought that was a wonderful idea and looked at the farmer anxiously.

"Well, let them stay if you want to," said Mr Taylor. "I'm not wanting to dress and go out at this time of night! We'll telephone to the Manor early tomorrow morning, before the children are missed."

So that night the children curled up in soft goose-feather beds at the Taylors' farm. They were very excited and very tired, but very, very happy. They didn't care what Mr Potts said, the treasure was theirs!

CHAPTER 19

GOOD LUCK TO GREYLINGS!

The children's grandparents were astonished when the telephone rang early the next morning and the news was told to them. At first they couldn't understand what had happened, but when they heard Laura's voice on the phone, telling them that they had found the Greylings Treasure, the two old people sat down and stared at one another in amazement.

Mr Taylor told his wife to give the children some breakfast, but for once the children were really too excited to eat anything. They swallowed down the creamy coffee that kind Mrs Taylor made, and then begged the farmer to take them home.

They were afraid of meeting Mr Potts on the way home. They wanted to get the treasure safely to Greylings Manor, so Mr Taylor brought his car up to the front door.

He and Nick put the box in the car boot.

Then they said goodbye to Mrs Taylor and climbed into the car themselves. They drove out of the farmyard and down Cuckoo Lane.

Gran and Grandad were waiting excitedly for the children. They could hardly believe it was true! They had telephoned a friend of Grandad's, an old man who was very knowledgeable about antiques and knew whether things were genuine or not. He had arrived just before the children came. His name was Mr Frost, and his hair was as white as his name. He, too, was very excited, for if the children really did have the old Greylings Treasure, it was a very remarkable find.

The car turned into the gates of Greylings Manor and drove up to the front steps. The children sprang out, and the farmer carried the old chest on his shoulder. Gran opened the door and the children rushed to meet her.

"Gran! We've got the treasure!"

"Gran! We've had such an adventure!"

"We've found the Greylings Treasure, Gran!"

"What a noise!" said Gran, and she led

the way to the study, where Mr Frost sat talking to Grandad. Grandad had taken out the old book that showed the treasure, and he and Mr Frost were examining the pictures carefully.

Mr Taylor put the old wooden box gently down on the table. "It's been in the pigsty," he said, with his large smile. "I'm afraid it doesn't smell very nice."

Nobody cared about that! Grandad flung back the lid and everyone looked inside. For the moment there wasn't a sound to be heard. Then, to everyone's surprise, Gran began to cry! She cried quite quietly, and the tears rolled down her soft pink cheeks one after another.

"What's the matter, Gran?" asked Laura in alarm, putting her arms round the old lady.

"Nothing, dear – just tears of happiness," said Gran. "It's extraordinary! Just as we were about to sell Greylings, you find the treasure!"

Mr Frost looked quite amazed. With his long thin fingers he took first one thing and then another out of the box. Soon the table was covered with precious jewels, and the wonderful golden cup shone in the midst of them.

"Yes," said Mr Frost, in a low voice, "yes! This is all old – very old. Wonderful stuff. Marvellous! And to think it has remained unspoilt and undiscovered all these years!"

"Is it worth a lot of money?" asked Laura.

"It's worth a fortune!" said Mr Frost. "It's almost priceless! This cup alone is worth thousands of pounds."

"Ooooh!" said the children, and looked with wide eyes at the dull gold of the carved cup, with its precious rubies and sapphires glowing around it.

"But I shan't sell it," said Grandad. "The famous Greyling Cup, found after so many years! It's unbelievable! The lucky cup is back where it belongs!"

"Gran, you won't have to sell Greylings now, will you?" asked Laura.

"No, we shan't," said Gran. "We shan't have to leave our beautiful home, it will be your father's – and yours – and your children's!"

"Mr Potts said that it was his, last

night," said Nick. "I knew he wasn't telling the truth."

"Well, he almost was," said Grandad. "Except for my signing one document, and Mr Potts signing another, the sale was complete. I'm not sure even now that we may not have some difficulty in withdrawing from the sale. We'll see what our solicitor says."

"It seems to me that this man's strange behaviour will tell against him when your solicitor hears about it," said Mr Frost suddenly. He had listened very carefully to all that the children had said. "I think, Mr Greyling, that you will find Mr Potts will not want anything said about his behaviour, and will not make any trouble."

"He did make Nick fall into the lake," said Katie. "We're sure of that."

"Yes. He is not a charming friend to have at all!" said Mr Frost. "I'll be interested to hear what he has to say about all this."

Laura, who had been listening impatiently to all the talk, suddenly went quite mad! "But we've got the treasure, the treasure, the treasure!" she yelled, spinning round like a top. "Nobody can take that away from us! It's ours, it belongs to the Greylings! Hurray! Hurray!"

She picked up two pearl necklaces and hung them round her neck. She pinned on two enormous brooches. She put a glittering bracelet round her wrist, and took the golden cup into her hand. "I've got the treasure! I've got the treasure," she sang, and danced round the room again. Everyone watched her and laughed.

Just at that moment the door opened, and Jane showed in Mr Potts and his solicitor! Laura almost bumped into them. Mr Potts stared at Laura in amazement when he saw all the jewellery she wore.

"The Greylings Treasure!" he snarled. "So you did find it after all! I began to think last night, when we hunted round the farm for it, that you had made up the tale of finding it just to annoy us!"

"It was in the pigsty, the pigsty, the pigsty!" chanted Laura.

Mr Potts suddenly remembered Gran and Grandad and bowed stiffly to them.

"I have brought my solicitor to hand you my cheque for Greylings," he said. "And, Mr Greyling, as your property is now mine,

I also claim the Greylings Treasure."

The children held their breath. What would Grandad say to that?

Grandad looked at Mr Potts very calmly. "I'm afraid," he said, "that there will be no sale. I can't accept your cheque, as now that the treasure has been found, there is no need for me to part with Greylings Manor. I very much regret that you have been put to so much unnecessary trouble. I shall be pleased to pay you whatever sum our solicitors agree upon to make up for the inconvenience and expense you have been put to."

"But this won't do, this won't do at all!" said Mr Potts, in a rage. "You can't get away with this! I'll soon show you that you can't behave like this to me!"

"Mr Potts," said Grandad in a voice like icy-cold water, "if I have any nonsense from you, my solicitors will hear these children's story of your very peculiar behaviour this last week; and I do not think you will want that made public. I feel very glad that Greylings Manor is not going to belong to your family. I think, if I may say so, that it deserves a better fate!"

Mr Potts listened to all this with a furious face. He went red and then white and then red again. He tried to speak. He swallowed hard. He looked as if he were going to burst, and then, with a noise that sounded like the squawk of an angry hen, he stamped from the room. His solicitor followed him, looking worried.

The front door banged. There was the noise of a car being started up. It sounded as angry as Mr Potts had looked.

Then the car roared off down the drive and everyone heaved a sigh of relief.

"Horrible man!" said Katie.

"I feel rather guilty about him," said Grandad. "The sale was almost complete, and I would have considered myself bound to go on with it, if it had been any other man. But I have heard such strange tales about Mr Potts lately that I am convinced he is not the right owner for Greylings. Now that I have heard how he has scared you children, and tried to get his hands on the treasure before the sale was completed, I am glad we have defeated him!"

"Oh, Gran! Oh, Grandad! Isn't everything lovely!" cried Laura, who was still wearing a great deal of jewellery. "I'm so happy! Greylings belongs to the Greylings for ever! What will Dad say when he hears that it's safe? Now we'll all be able to stay here as often as we like!"

"You certainly will!" said Gran, hugging the excited little girl. "And how very glad I am that Nick and Katie have joined our family. You would never have been able to find the treasure on your own, Laura. You all deserve a reward for being so clever!"

"We've got our reward," said Nick. "We've found the treasure for you. Oh, Gran, it was such fun hunting for it! You nearly stopped us finding it yesterday though, when you sent us to our rooms!"

"Poor children!" said Gran. "No wonder you were late for lunch! You should have told us all that you were doing, and then we would have understood!"

"But it was great fun having a secret," said Katie.

"Woof!" said Russet, who had been quite bewildered by all the excitement. He had hidden under the table, and now he came out and licked Nick's legs.

"Russet was a great help, Gran!" said

Laura, patting the little dog. "We couldn't have done without him."

"I think," said Grandad, beaming round at everyone, "I think that such an exciting day needs a celebration – and naturally I include Russet in that invitation. What about going out to the ice-cream shop and ordering the largest and most delicious ices they have?"

"Oooh, yes!" shouted the children, and off they all went to eat chocolate, strawberry and vanilla ices. And what do you think Grandad did? He took with him the Greylings Cup and had it filled with iced lemonade at the shop!

"Now we must all drink from the lucky cup!" he said. "Just as the Greylings did many years ago. And each year we must meet and drink from it again, and we'll hope that good fortune and happiness will come to every member of the Greylings family – and that means you, Nick, and you Katie, and your children too."

Then all of them drank from the cup and said the same words – "Good luck to Greylings Manor – and may it always belong to a Greyling!"